BORROWED ISLAND

Forty-Two Stories from A Visitor Who Forgot to Leave

Randip Sahu

Sabre & Quill

Published by
Sabre & Quill Publishers, New Delhi, India
www.sabreandquill.com
sabreandquill@gmail.com

Distributed by
Bookmart Distributors, Bhikaji Cama Place, New Delhi-110066
Tel: +91-11-26193636/ Handset: +91-9810700039
email: bookmart329@gmail.com

First Published: **2025**

Printed in BHARAT

All illustrations are drawn from the author's private photographic collection and select AI-generated images used under the author's direction.

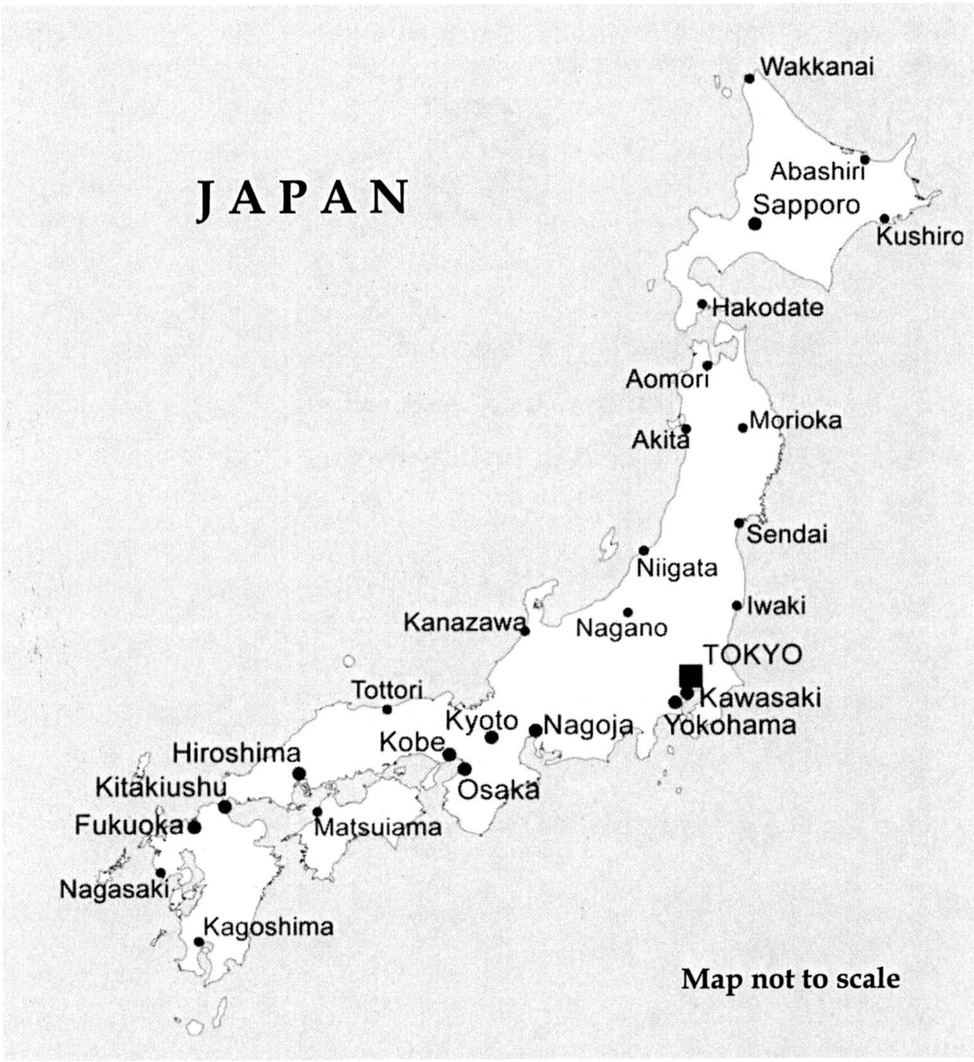
JAPAN
Wakkanai
Abashiri
Sapporo
Kushiro
Hakodate
Aomori
Akita
Morioka
Sendai
Niigata
Iwaki
Kanazawa
Nagano
TOKYO
Kawasaki
Yokohama
Tottori
Kyoto
Nagoja
Kobe
Hiroshima
Osaka
Kitakiushu
Fukuoka
Matsuiama
Nagasaki
Kagoshima
Map not to scale

Beauty needs no scaffolding.
It moves us to admiration.
True beauty, like the sun,
does not reflect—it radiates.
And when it shines,
it moves us not to admiration,
but to tears of joy.

Contents

Foreword ix

Author's Reflection xi

Acknowledgements xv

Introduction xvii

Section I: Staged Affections, True Feelings

1. Echoes in Three Lines: Appreciation and Writing Haiku 2
2. Rental Hearts in a Disposable Age 8
3. The Woman Who Forgot to Return 12

Section II: Portals and Thresholds: The Sacred and the Vanishing

4. Under the Torii Gates 17
5. Shinto Shrines: Where Absence Becomes Presence 21
6. Obon: Where the Dead Return Gently Home 28
7. The Homing Dead 34
8. Noh Theatre: Masks That Remember the Wind 38
9. Balancing Shinto and Zen 44
10. The Seven Japanese Paths to the Summit 49

Section III: Memory, Resistance, and the Shadows of History

11. The Ghost in the Pachinko Machine 57

12. Naoko's Monologue 64

13. Japan's Ancient to Modern History and Politics 69

14. Japan's Quiet Transformation 75

15. Japanese Film, Architecture, and Literature 81

16. Rento Rikitake Returns Home 86

17. Hiroshima 90

18. Japan, Don't Cry for Me 100

19. Ink, Not Blood 107

Section IV: Creatures of Sign and Whimsy

20. The Cultural Reign of the Cat 114

21. A Tale of Two Tails and Two Royalties 118

22. The Enigmatic Japanese Toy 124

Section V: Neon Pulse — The Machinery of Modern Life

23. The Salaryman 130

24. Benjiro Bushimata Misses the 7:46 a.m. Train 135

25. The Yakuza 139

26. The Hot Cigarette Burns on Cold Skin 144

27. All That Glitters Is Gold in Dōtonbori 150

28. Vegetarian in Japan 155

29. The Midnight Diner 160

30. Happy Hour in Tokyo 166
31. The Piss Alley Rebellion, Tokyo 170

Section VI: Horse, Sword, and Wind

32. The Wrestler and the Weight of Wind 178
33. The Japanese Racetrack as Ritual and Theatre 183
34. Chasing Phantoms 188

Section VII: Time-Torn Futures and Generational Echoes

35. Bushidō 196
36. Swordsmiths of Light and Shadow 201
37. The Last Code 206
38. Gothic Lolita, Cosplay, and Vivid Dreams 213
39. The Lovers Who Never Were 218
40. The Parable of Three Vending Machines 222

Section VIII: Lanterns for the Way Ahead

41. Japan's Sacred Symbols 227
42. The God of Small Things 235

Epilogue 240

Appendix A: Popular Tourist Spots: Tokyo 244
Appendix B: Popular Tourist Spots: Kyoto 247
Appendix C: Popular Tourist Spots: Osaka 250
Appendix D: Popular Tourist Spots: Hiroshima 253
Appendix E: Useful Addresses for the Vegetarian Travellers 256

Appendix F: Glossary of Japanese Words and Phrases 259
Appendix G: Sixteen Days Across Japan: A Recommended Itinerary 264

Foreword

Some books inform. Others linger—like a half-heard melody that never fades. *Borrowed Island: Forty-Two Stories From a Visitor Who Forgot to Leave* belongs to the latter kind.

Randip Sahu's writing is distinguished by lyrical precision and an interior stillness. This is a work that listens before it speaks. Here, Japan is not displayed but revealed—quietly, patiently, with reverence for both the visible and the invisible.

What makes this book remarkable is its layered form. Certain essays stand whole in themselves; others are accompanied by "Twin Echoes"—fictional counterparts that deepen their emotional and philosophical textures. These are not echoes of repetition, but of resonance: spirals where truth and imagination entwine.

Randip writes with patience and clarity. Whether he is tracing the role of cats and dogs in culture, a salaryman's ritual solitude, or the silences of Hiroshima, he allows each moment its full gravity.

This is no guidebook. It is a companion—a meditation. A quiet pact with the places that altered him—and that may alter you.

You need not pack a bag; the voyage awaits you in the following paragraphs. He has shaped these pages so you can travel without leaving your seat, and return changed. Read, and let the islands rise around you like mist—no borders, only wonder. Here the world unfolds inward: landscapes of ink and memory that ask only your attention, not your ticket.

You may close these pages, but something of this island will remain with you. Just as its author, in spirit, never truly left.

Virender Kapoor
Author, Educator, Leadership Coach

Author's Reflection

"Were it not for shadows, there would be no beauty."

—Jun'ichirō Tanizaki

Why *Borrowed Island*?
Why not *The Borrowed Island*, you might ask?

The omission is deliberate. To add, "The" word would pin to geography, to a fixed coordinate, to a labelled place on a map. But *Borrowed Island* is not a *destination*. It is a *condition*. A quiet enchantment cast by a country that—for a moment, or a decade—allows you entry, teaches you to walk differently, to bow more precisely, to sit inside silence. And then, without asking permission, it *rewires* your sense of time, meaning, and even the etiquette of chopsticks.

The island is "borrowed" not in the colonial sense (heaven forbid), nor in the sense of souvenirs (though I must confess to a drawer full of *wasabi*—a pungent Japanese horseradish—tubes and *matcha*—ground green tea powder—tins). It is borrowed in the way waking life *borrows from a dream: briefly yours, yet permanently altering you.*

This title is my acknowledgement of the visitor's gentle intrusion—my own. I arrived in Japan briefly but departed slowly, carrying with me brushstrokes of *shodō* (Japanese calligraphy), the faint incense of *Obon* (a Buddhist festival that honours the spirit of ancestors) altars, and the hush of temple courtyards. These forty-two stories—ranging from cultural essays and narratives to short fiction and quiet metaphysical puzzles—trace that impression. They reflect a Japan glimpsed through a *torii gate* (traditional Shinto shrine gateway or portal symbolising the transition from the mundane to the sacred) at dusk, from the back window of a bullet train, or during a 7:46 a.m. commute beside a man who has perfected the art of sleeping while standing.

Each section of this book explores a different aspect of that "borrowedness": language and resistance, sacred thresholds and vending machines, *yakuza* (members of organised crime syndicates in Japan) tattoos and silent shrines, *pachinko* (an arcade gambling slot machine) ghosts and wind-borne warriors, children of after-everything futures.

Together, they create not a guidebook but a borrowed map—drawn in chalk, not ink—of an unseen Japan. One you enter, not through arrival halls but through a willingness to forget yourself a little. And perhaps, not entirely leave.

And just when I believed the journey was complete, the sacred piece arrived—not from study or reason, but from silence. One morning, as I walked alone through the thousand vibrant red tori gates leading up to Mount Inari at Fushimi-Inari Taisha Temple in Kyoto, in the southern Fushimi Ward, I felt the air shift. The body knew before the mind. The seven Japanese principles (*"The Seven Japanese Paths to Summit"*) I had studied—*Ikigai, Shikata ga nai, Wabi-sabi, Gaman, Oubaitori, Kaizen, and Shuhari*—ceased to be abstract ideals. They revealed themselves as companions I had been carrying all along. That piece wrote itself.

For readers' ease, Japanese words and phrases appear in italics, accompanied by an English translation whenever possible. After that first introduction, those words are set in regular (roman) type for subsequent appearances, while any terms without immediate translations are gathered alphabetically in the Glossary at the end of the book.

The book is an expedition of the mind: no passport, no luggage, only the willingness to journey.

Further, the book is less a conclusion than an act of quiet attention. Thank you for coming this far. May the following pages not resolve your questions, but change their shape.

So yes, I forgot to leave.
And *Borrowed Island* is what remains.

Randip Sahu

09 November 2025
Pune

Acknowledgements

This book began long before the first word was written or the first suitcase packed. It began in conversations and in longing, in the quiet plotting of days to come—shaped by the kindness, patience, and insight of many, each adding their own shade to these pages.

My deepest gratitude belongs to my daughter, Ipshita, whose vision, precision, and quiet brilliance turned a dream of Japan into a lived reality. For nearly a year, she choreographed our journey with care, threading temples and tea houses, alleyways and art museums, *ryokans* (traditional Japanese inns or lodgings), and ramen stalls—guiding us through a symphony of buses, bullet trains, and unexpected wonders. From Michelin-starred marvels to hidden *machiya* (traditional Japanese townhouse) tucked away on Airbnb, she shepherded us—single-handedly—across a country and into its heartbeat. Her technical acumen, instincts, and unfailing backup plans formed the invisible scaffolding of this book. Ipshita, thank you—for every map, every miracle, every moment.

To my wife, Sulotika, I owe a quieter, yet no less profound, debt. Her unflagging support and luminous companionship steadied me across unfamiliar landscapes, and—more remarkably still—she granted me the solitude to write when we returned. With patience, encouragement, and a generosity of silence, she held the stillness in which these stories could take form.

I remain indebted to Col. Virender Kapoor—prolific writer, educator, and mentor—for the generous gift of his Foreword.

To Nobu Nakamura—translator, storyteller, and friend—your laughter, patience, and perception walk softly through these chapters.

My heartfelt thanks extend also to Sabre & Quill Publishers and their gifted team, who transformed a wayward manuscript into the illustrated book now in your hands. Their faith, their keen editorial eye, and their devotion to detail shaped *Borrowed Island: Forty-Two Stories From a Visitor Who Forgot To Leave* into something more coherent, more luminous, than I could have created alone.

To the many unnamed companions of this journey—researchers, librarians, curators, monks, guides, chefs, and hotel staff—your insights and hospitality ripple quietly beneath the surface of these pages.

And to the random strangers encountered along the way—the late-night patrons of *izakayas* (Japanese bar or tavern that serve alcoholic beverages and snacks, similar to tapas bars in Spain or pubs in the West), the spectators at wrestling rings and racecourses, the silent fellow travellers waiting on platforms or passing through narrow lanes—thank you. You reminded me that the soul of a place often reveals itself unannounced, in a fleeting glance, in laughter shared, in gestures too brief to record yet too human to forget.

Sometimes it takes a borrowed island to return you to parts of yourself you never knew were missing.

Introduction

Some visitors arrive politely: they slip off their shoes, sip the tea, bow their thanks, and leave.
And then there are those who… forget.

This book belongs to the second kind. *Borrowed Island: Forty-Two Stories From a Visitor Who Forgot to Leave* is neither memoir nor reportage. It is a quiet act of narrative trespass—part cultural essay, part personal parable, part fiction, part meditation. Think of it as lingering in Japan's genkan: pausing for one more question, noticing one more cat, following one more lantern down an alley where the real story hides behind the steam of ramen.

Blending travel, philosophy, memoir, and storytelling, these pages offer a soul's-eye view of Japan—through its shrines and side streets, its silent revolutions and unspoken meanings. Much in Japan resides not in what is declared, but in what remains unsaid.

The work unfolds in eight thematic movements, including Staged Affection, True Feelings, Lanterns for the Way Ahead, and others. Within this structure lies an experiment: a hybrid form pairing essay with short fiction. In the table of section contents, such pairings are marked with an asterisk (*); in the text, they are linked by a diamond (❖), the fiction additionally noted as "Twin Echo to [Title]"—a visual cue for the dialogue between the two. This is not a device but a way of seeing: a double helix where truth and imagination entwine, creating something fuller and more enduring—an echo that lingers after the page is turned.

Interwoven with these paired essays and "Twin Echo" fictions are three larger constellations—Triptych of Fire, Silence, and Renewal, Triptych of Quiet Honour, and Triptych of Vivid Youth.

The first, the Triptych of Fire, Silence, and Renewal, moves from the searing flash of *Hiroshima* to the quiet lament of *Japan, "Don't Cry for Me," and finally to the gentle insistence of "Ink, Not Blood,"* tracing a single arc of human resilience.

The second, the Triptych of Quiet Honour, gathers three reflections on the unseen life of the code: *Bushidō* offers the philosophical foundation; *Swordsmiths of Light and Shadow* embodies it in craft and lineage; *The Last Code* moves the theme into a contemporary—or even futuristic—register, showing what remains when the world tries to forget.

The third, the Triptych of Vivid Youth, follows the restless imagination of Japan's Gen Z—a generation inventing itself in the space between inheritance and reinvention. *Gothic Lolita, Cosplay, and Vivid Dreams* explores the performative aspects of identity and fashion as a form of liberation. *The Lovers Who Never Were* turns to the private, dreamlike interior lives of young relationships. *The Parable of Three Vending Machines* reflects their consumer landscape and the playful, surreal edge of their daily world. Together, these triptychs form a quiet resonance within the book's larger conversation—meditations on fidelity, silence, and self-invention that cross centuries.

Some examples of the book's paired form:

- *Obon: Where the Dead Return Gently Home* is mirrored by *The Homing Dead,* where return is ritual, not haunting.
- *The Salaryman Misses the 7:46 a.m. Train* finds its echo in *Benjiro Bushimata,* lending emotional weight to Tokyo's clockwork rhythm.

This is not a guidebook. It is a contemplative map—drawn in brushstrokes and bent neon, traced in the space between memory and myth.

I have tried to craft the stories so that you don't leave your seat.

❄

Section I:

Staged Affections, True Feelings

Meaning in Japan is often sculpted not from abundance, but from absence. This section turns toward two forms where constraint becomes revelation: the pared-down world of *haiku* (the Japanese poetic form that captures a fleeting moment), and the choreographed intimacies of companionship for hire. In both, feeling is framed within fixed boundaries—seventeen syllables, or a prepaid hour. Yet within those limits, something unexpectedly honest may appear. A haiku holds its silence as carefully as its words; a hired partner offers a warmth rehearsed, but not always false. Each moment, though composed, still asks to be lived—if only for the span of a breath.

Contents

1 Echoes in Three Lines: Appreciation and Writing Haiku

2 Rental Hearts in a Disposable Age ★

3 The Woman Who Forgot to Return ★

❄

Echoes in Three Lines: Appreciation and Writing Haiku

The wind lifts a sleeve –
bamboo shadows cross the path,
time bows, then vanishes.

It began one warm afternoon above Arashiyama, near Tenryu-ji Temple, located in the western suburbs of Kyoto, known for its stunning natural beauty, including the iconic Bamboo Grove. Our guide, Yamamoto-san, paused mid-trail as though listening to a sound only he could hear. He tapped his stick on a stone, and in the hush that followed said: *"That is kigo in nature."*

A season word, he explained—not just a name, but a gesture. A cicada is not merely an insect; it is summer itself. A crow silhouetted against a pale sky is winter embodied. In haiku, the world does not decorate the poem; it inhabits it.

I had always thought of haiku as form: three lines, five-seven-five syllables, a neat miniature. But standing in the breath of bamboo, I began to see it differently. Haiku is less about constructing than noticing. It is a stillness caught just before it vanishes.

Three elements lie quietly beneath most haiku:

- ❄ *Kigo*: the season distilled into a word or image.
- ❄ *Kireji*: a subtle cut or pause, a shift of perception.
- ❄ *Ma*: the silence between things, where meaning ripens.

Yamamoto-san read one of his poems to us, not as instruction but as offering:

Quiet hillside pond –
a stone's circle fades outward,
soundless after-sound.

He smiled when he saw our puzzled faces. "Don't try to be profound," he said. "Try to be attentive."

That was his only lesson. Haiku, he reminded us, is not a river of thought but a drop of dew. It vanishes, yet leaves the taste of sky.

I began, awkwardly, to write one of my own. He neither praised nor corrected—he simply nodded, as though beginnings were sacred too.

Haiku is not a subject to be mastered. It is a way of seeing. A bow at a station, a child's nose wiped with a sleeve, a camellia in a shadowed alcove—each could be a poem, if we look long enough.

Not every leaf becomes a verse. But every verse was once a leaf.

✦ Yamamoto-san's Pocket Guide to Writing Haiku ✦

He folds his hands, eyes bright with quiet humour. "Haiku," he begins, "is less about rules than about attention. But a few simple steps will help you begin."

❆ Notice something small.
"Look carefully," he says, letting the room fall still.
"A drifting leaf, a cooling teacup, a bird startled into flight—
these small moments are the gateways."

❆ Anchor it in the season.
"This is the *kigo*," he explains.
"A single word or image—snow, cicada, blossom, frost—
that carries the breath of time itself."

❆ Let the shift happen.
"Most haiku hold a gentle turn, the *kireji*,"
he continues, making a slight pivot with his hand.
"One image gives way to another,
and in that contrast, surprise is born."

❆ Keep it brief.
"In Japanese we speak of five–seven–five," he smiles,
"but in English, shorter lines with a natural rhythm serve best.
Say only what is needed."

❆ Feel the *ma*.
He closes his eyes for a heartbeat.
"The silence between images is part of the poem.
Let the pause breathe so the reader can enter."

❆ Leave space.
"Haiku is not a conclusion but an opening," he says softly.
"The poem ends only when it reaches the reader."

He turns to the blackboard and writes, slowly:

Observe → Anchor → Shift → Breathe (*ma*) → Subtract → Offer

"Now," he adds, tapping the word *Subtract*,
"this is where many poets falter."

On Subtraction

"It is not arithmetic," Yamamoto-san explains.
"It is the art of letting go."

❆ Cut the excess words.
"Remove anything that tells instead of shows.
If one image carries the feeling,
you need no explaining adjective."

❆ Trust the reader's imagination.
"Haiku thrives on implication.
Leave space for the reader to hear the sound,
feel the motion, sense the emotion."

❆ Honour impermanence.
"This act of release reflects the spirit of haiku itself—
the beauty of what remains unsaid."

He lays down the chalk.
"Observe fully. Feel the pause.
Then remove everything that is not essential.
Only then do you offer the finished poem."

The room is quiet; even the paper seems to hold its breath.
You can almost hear the wind moving through the ink.

✦ From Yamamoto-san's private collection ✦

He offers his haiku and its interpretation:

Ink pools in silence—
a single stroke becomes wind,
paper holds its breath.

He places the sheet before us and smiles.
"This," he says, "is how I feel each time I lift the brush."

Reading the images

Ink pools in silence—
"Before the brush moves," Yamamoto-san explains, "the inkstone is heavy with quiet.
This is *ma*—the living pause before action, a moment dense with possibility."

a single stroke becomes wind,
"When the brush finally touches paper, the line is no longer mere ink.

It moves like a sudden gust, a reminder that art is not only something we see, but something that happens."

paper holds its breath.
"Even the page seems to wait," he continues, "as if aware that a fleeting instant has been fixed forever.
It is the hush that follows creation."

What it shows us

"The poem follows the rhythm of making: poised stillness, a single burst of motion, then the quiet after," Yamamoto-san concludes. "Haiku lives in that balance. What remains unsaid—the breath the paper keeps—is as important as the mark itself."

He bows slightly.
"Begin not with wisdom, but with attentiveness.
The rest will arrive like wind in the ink."

❄

❖ Rental Hearts in a Disposable Age

Cherry blossoms fall –
a rented smile lingers near,
real as it must be.

In the still hum of a Tokyo café, I once overheard what sounded like the gentlest breakup in the world.

“I had a wonderful time today,” she said, bowing ever so slightly, as one does here even at the edge of sadness

The man across from her, neatly dressed, nodded with a grateful smile—too composed, too symmetrical for heartbreak. They left in opposite directions. Neither turned back.

Only later did I learn they were not lovers at all. She had been rented. He had hired her.

Japan’s rent-a-person industry is often reduced to “rent-a-girlfriend” or “rent-a-family,” but it is something more intricate: a theatre of intimacy. Clients hire not for sex or romance, but for the semblance of companionship. A boyfriend at a reunion. A daughter to accompany an ageing parent. A father figure at a wedding. They are not actors in the conventional sense, but purveyors of presence.

Boundaries are strict: no unscripted contact, no continuation beyond the contract. Yet the performance often looks indistinguishable from tenderness.

Why seek a rented heart in a country famed for courtesy? Part of the answer lies in Japan's social architecture. *Tatemae* (harmony) is prized above *honne* (raw feeling). The appearance of a well-lived life can matter as much as the reality. And so, if a middle-aged woman needs a fiancé to bring home for New Year's, or a shy office worker wishes to practice kindness, there is someone available—for a fee.

Even the queer community, negotiating conservative expectations, finds unexpected refuge here. A gay man may hire a female partner to attend a cousin's wedding. A transgender woman might rent a "brother" to stand beside her at a family event. These roles are not deception so much as survival.

Agencies like Family Romance or OSSAN Rental (specialising in older men as companions or advisers) function as digital storefronts of persona. For ¥8,000 to ¥15,000 an hour ($60–$110), one can purchase a slice of warmth—calibrated, contained, performed with grace.

But tenderness cannot be faked forever without cost. Werner Herzog's film *Family Romance, LLC* traces this ambiguity: a man hired to impersonate an absent father finds both he and the child growing attached, until the boundary between act and reality begins to dissolve.

Workers in this field often speak of exhaustion, and some even experience heartbreak. One rent-a-daughter recalled attending the funeral of a client's mother: "I was supposed to be her daughter. But I wasn't allowed to cry." What does it mean when grief itself is forbidden, because the bond was never "real"?

Yet in Japan, substitution has long been ritualised. From the choreographies of the tea ceremony to the pageantry of sumo, role and performance are not deceit, but structure. In an age of shrinking families, long work hours, and loneliness so common that it has its own word, kodokushi (dying alone), perhaps these rented relationships are less an anomaly than a necessity—emotional scaffolding in a fragile society.

And perhaps the line between performance and presence is thinner than we admit. After all, when someone listens to your story, laughs at your joke, and meets your eyes with what looks like care, does it matter that you paid them to be there?

Some clients hire the same person for years: to walk beneath the cherry blossoms each spring, to mark a birthday with the same father figure each autumn. A contract binds them at first. Later, only habit—and something harder to name—remains.

On my last visit to Tokyo, I returned to that café. The doors opened and closed like stage curtains. I recognised one of the "girlfriends" from an article. She poured tea, leaned forward, and laughed at a joke that seemed real. Perhaps it was.

We all, in some way, perform love.
Some simply do it with clearer terms –
and a receipt.

❄

❖ The Woman Who Forgot to Return

(*Twin Echo to Rental Hearts in a Disposable Age*)

Empty park bench waits –
wax drips into ruined sweetness,
no one blows it out.

The first time Kenji hired her, it was spring. The city smelled of thawing rain, cherry petals dragging across wet pavements.

She arrived in a pale blue cardigan, hair tied in a loose knot. "Shall we?" she asked softly, as though the script had been written on the air between them.

They walked the river path where lanterns swayed above izakaya doors. He told her about the ramen shop he had loved as a student, about how the broth had changed. She listened, nodding, eyes wide enough to make it seem she cared.

"Do you like spring?" he asked finally.

"I like beginnings," she replied, without hesitation.

He didn't tell her that for him, spring always felt like an ending.

The second time was summer. They met in a café near Shinjuku Station, cicadas rasping outside like iron wires. She ordered iced coffee. He asked for tea.

"You look tired," she said.

"I am." He meant more than she could know.

Her smile was practised, but her pause afterwards was not. "You don't have to talk today, if you'd rather not."

They sat in silence. Two strangers in a crowd, holding the illusion of familiarity.

When they parted, she bowed. "Take care."

The words sounded real. Maybe they were.

By autumn, the appointments had become a season of their own. He booked her for his birthday. They shared cake on a park bench, leaves falling like broken coins around them.

"Make a wish," she said, holding a candle-lit slice.

"I already have."

He didn't blow out the candle. He let it burn until the wax dripped on the frosting, a small ruin in the middle of sweetness. She looked away.

"Sometimes," she whispered, "I wish I could stay."

But the script allowed no improvisations.

Winter arrived like a blade.

His mother had been gone for years, yet the anniversary still cut clean as paper. He hired her to accompany him to the cemetery. She stood beside him, coat collar turned high against the wind that scraped the air raw.

"She was kind?" she asked.

"Yes."

"And strict?"

"Very."

She bowed to the gravestone as though the gesture might reach the dead. "Then she raised you well."

Something cracked in his throat. "She would have liked you."

The words escaped before he could catch them.

They hung there, fragile as a lantern in a winter gust. She tightened her scarf, eyes lowered. "Please don't," she whispered, the plea soft as frost.

The last time was never on any calendar. Months later, along the same river path where they had first met, he saw her again—arm in arm with another client, her laughter falling lightly, like rain on glass. Kenji slowed. She looked up, met his gaze, and for the length of a breath her smile faltered before settling back into its practised curve. Neither spoke. In his pocket lay the dried petals he had carried through seasons. He let them slip into the gutter, the wind lifting them like pale, harmless lies.

That night, he wrote her name—not her real name, but the agency's: Yuzuki, gentle moon. He walked the moonlit river's edge, watching the current cradle leaves and an unlikely scrap of folded paper. His fist tightened around the small page until its edges cut his palm. He raised it towards the black water, imagining the paper spinning away, imagining the loss he already carried. Then, almost without thought, he folded it once, then again, and slid it back into his wallet.

Not because she belonged to him, not because she knew her name, but because for a handful of rented hours she had seemed to—close enough to believe, too far ever to keep.

❄

Section II:

Portals and Thresholds: The Sacred and the Vanishing

Where passage is not merely movement but transformation, this section navigates spaces shaped by silence, ritual, and reverence. A torii is not a gate but a crossing. A shrine is not a place, but a presence—even the dead return—not to haunt, but to remind.

Here, the sacred does not arrive with a pronouncement. It lingers, flickers, and vanishes—just slowly enough to be glimpsed: in the curve of a Noh mask that remembers the wind, in the footfall on a mountain path that leads both upward and inward, in the smoke of incense that dissolves into summer dusk. These are thresholds more felt than seen, reminding us that the invisible may be the most enduring.

Contents

4 Under the Torii Gates

5 Shintō Shrines: Where Absence Becomes Presence

6 Obon: Where the Dead Return Gently Home ★

7 The Homing Dead ★

8 Noh Theatre: Masks that Remember the Wind

9 Balancing Shintō and Zen ★

10 The Seven Japanese Paths to Summit ★

❄

Under the Torii Gates

Beneath red silence
a question steps through the morning –
the gate does not close.

Kyoto, May 2025

The rain had passed, but its breath still lingered—soft and damp—over the gravel path rising behind the shrine. I had woken before dawn, not from discipline but from a restlessness I could not name.

I followed a faint trail through cedar and mist, and there it was: a vermilion Torii gate, standing solitary, the forest threading itself like a loom around its arch.

That's when he appeared. A monk in grey, drawn from the folds of morning. He looked at me calmly, and for a moment the birdsong fell silent.

"You are already inside," he said.

"Inside what?"

He pointed to the gate above us, the line of red against pale mist.

"Inside the question."

The Gate as Gesture

We walked together, not with a destination but with a rhythm. Each step on gravel was punctuation, each silence a page turned.

The Torii, I realised, was neither a barrier nor an entrance. It was a slowing down, an invitation to cross with attention.

"In your world," the monk said, "answers come quickly. Here, we practice the moment before."

It was the first time I felt the weight of a pause, a silence that had decided to speak.

Tea and the Invisible Thread

Later, we sat beneath a sloping roof, cups of matcha steaming between us. Rain returned, light and undecided, carrying the scent of wet cedar.

I asked about ma, the space between things.

"It is not absence," he said. "Ma is the presence of what waits—the breath before it leaves, the pause that lets the mountain hold still in a painting."

He tapped the table lightly.

"That space is where the sacred hides."

I thought of my week: bullet-train timetables, top-ten lists, angles designed for Instagram. I had arrived with questions, but left no room for them to echo.

Ritual as Reverence

That afternoon, he showed me how to bow at a shrine—not as performance, but as attention. The ladle of water was lifted like part of a conversation.

"The kami do not ask for perfection," he said. "Only sincerity."

There were no commandments, no sermon. Just gestures, slow and deliberate: wash, clap twice, bow, release. Ritual, I understood then, is not repetition. It is listening.

Emptiness, Without Lack

At a small temple near Arashiyama, I joined a zazen group. We sat in silence before a raked gravel garden, stones arranged as if someone had listened to them first. My knees ached, my mind wandered—but something rearranged inside me.

Later, I asked, "Why is emptiness such a goal in Zen?"

The monk smiled gently.

"Emptiness is not lack. It is clarity. Like water settling when left undisturbed."

He gestured toward the garden.

"That stone does not need meaning. But your mind will give it one. Zen is noticing—before the meaning."

Leaving Without Leaving

The next morning, I returned to the Torii gate. Light streamed through the branches; the path was dry, but the gate itself felt changed. Not a place I had passed through, but a state I had entered.

I bowed once, then left without words, carrying his last offering:

"You came for understanding. But perhaps you'll leave with reverence."

The Gate That Stays Open

Back in the city—among vending machines, train announcements, and glowing screens—I found myself seeking that space again. And slowly, I realised: I didn't need Kyoto for the gate. It was already with me.

The Torii is not only architecture. It is the pause between question and answer, between thought and breath—a way of walking through the world with reverence.

A gate that never closes.

❈

Shinto Shrines:

Where Absence Becomes Presence

No wind, yet leaves stir—
a gate with nothing behind,
and yet I enter.

The Torii That Waits

I had not intended to find the shrine.
Or perhaps the shrine had intended to find me.

It was just past dawn in a small town near Osaka. Fog drifted like incense among the hills. I set out with no map, only my camera and a restlessness I couldn't explain. My feet carried me down mossy lanes until I reached a vermilion torii, standing solitary in a clearing. No walls. No signs. Only the gate, and the silence beyond.

An old man swept the gravel path nearby. He looked up, sensing my hesitation—was I intruding, or had I arrived?

"It's alright," he said gently. "You don't need belief to enter. Just breathe."

"What is this place?" I asked.

He smiled faintly. "A place where something chooses not to show itself—yet remains."

Empty Spaces, Full of Meaning

I stepped through the torii. The air shifted, as though tuned to a softer frequency.

No idols, sermons, stained glass—none of these. Only stillness. A gravel courtyard. A cedar bound with sacred rope. A wooden offering box. A structure barely large enough to house a presence, if one chose to dwell there.

I understood: shrines do not instruct. They invite.

They are not religions of revelation, but of resonance.

Here, the divine dwells not above, but around—in wind, in water, in bark, in silence. In the absence that speaks.

A Woman and a Whisper

Later, by the basin of water for ritual cleansing, I met a young woman filling her hands with coolness. She wore modern clothes, but her movements carried an older rhythm.

“Do you come here often?” I asked.

“Only when I lose something,” she said.

“A person?”

She shook her head.

“Not always. Sometimes… part of myself.”

“And you find it here?”

“Sometimes. Sometimes I only hear where to look.”

Her name was Aiko. Before leaving, she wrote on an *ema* plaque and hung it under the eaves. I did not read it. I wouldn't have understood.

The Voice Beneath the Noise

Shrines in Tokyo hide in alleyways, like pockets of breath in a breathless city. In Kyoto, they float on lakes or crouch beneath mountains. Yet all seem to say the same word: *Listen.*

At Fushimi Inari, where ten thousand gates rise into the forest, I met a boy resting halfway up the hill, his backpack slumped like a stone.

"Do people climb all the way?" I asked.

"Yes," he said. "But not for the same reason."

"And yours?"

He pointed upward. "My grandfather said the gods hear better from high places."

"Do you believe him?"

The boy hesitated. "I don't know. But I still climb."

What the Shrines Taught Me

That night, I lit a single candle in my room. No bells, no chants. Only a pine branch I had picked up from the shrine floor, resting on the sill.

Shinto has no scripture. No commandments. No hell. Only *kami*—spirits unseen but sensed. They live in mirrors, foxes, stones, rice, rustling leaves.

Most of all, they live in invitation.

- To enter not because the space is full, but because it is cleared of clutter.
- To bow, not to a statue, but to the space between things.
- To listen, not for answers, but for presence.

Epilogue:

The gate is always there. Even now, in the noise of the city, the memory of that first torii remains. It is a gate to nothing.

It is a gate to everything.

And each time I close my eyes, I walk through again.

Empty shrine at dusk –
a single pine cone trembles.
The god says nothing.

Obon: Where the Dead Return Gently Home

Paper lantern floats –
even shadows know the path
back to warm doorways.

How I Heard the Silence of August

I was not in Japan in August. I was there in May, wandering temple paths, reading wooden plaques beneath cherry trees just beginning to forget their blossoms. But August found me anyway – through the quiet recollections of a man named Nobu Nakamura.

Nobu was my occasional translator, guide, and, by accident or fate, the stillest person I met in Japan. Just past fifty, soft-voiced, his glasses often fogged from tea too hot, he seemed to live in the pauses between words. He never interrupted the silence unless the silence asked for him.

We first met in Kyoto, waiting out a sudden rain beneath the awning of a bookstore. He was browsing Bashō; I was pretending not to shiver. By the time the rain cleared, we had agreed to share a route through old temples and small stations. Not quite friends, not quite strangers – we became what he once called "companion listeners."

It was during one of those slow walks through a Kyoto neighbourhood that he first mentioned Obon.

"The city changes in August," he said, stopping before a shuttered shop that sold incense and handmade dolls.

"How so?"

"It quiets itself. It bows to what is not here."

Stories Nobu Nakamura Told Me of Obon

Over barley tea in a tatami-matted teahouse, Nobu shared his memories—not performances, not cultural explanations, but gently folded recollections.

His father had died the summer he turned sixteen. Every August, his mother set an altar with his father's watch and work shoes. "Even now," Nobu said softly, "I half expect the shoes to move."

He spoke of his first *Bon Odori*, the communal dance of Obon. He had refused to go—too shy, too unsure of the steps. His grandfather told him, *"Don't worry. The dead will dance with you, if you let them lead."*

Later, passing a modest teahouse, he gestured quietly. "That's Fumiko-san's place. Her son never came back from Sapporo. She says that when the spirits arrive, the tatami creaks differently."

Nobu never urged me to write these things down. He only said, *"Let's go slowly today."*

A Lantern's Story, and the Boy Who Knew

One August evening by the Kamo River, Nobu had met a boy named Daichi, holding a lantern beside his grandmother, waiting for dusk. Lanterns would soon be floated downstream, guiding ancestral spirits home.

"Do you want to talk to them?" the boy asked.

"Them?"

"The ones you miss," the grandmother explained. "You whisper into the flame. The lantern knows the way."

When Nobu told me this, he paused, as though waiting for a name to rise. Then he whispered something too softly to catch. I didn't ask him to repeat it.

That night, I imagined Daichi's lantern trembling in his hands—its flame shy, determined, carrying words not spoken in years.

In the Mountains, the Fire Spells Goodbye

Nobu once joined the crowds at Kyoto's *Gozan Okuribi*—the five great bonfires lit on the mountains, each forming a vast kanji to send the spirits home.

He described the hush before the flames bloomed, the way a woman nearby whispered: *"We light it not because they are gone, but because we are still here."*

He did not linger on that story. He rarely lingered. He believed silence deserved its portion.

The Dead Return Gently, Even in May

Obon, as Nobu gave it to me, was not a festival to attend. It was a return to be received.

On my last day in Kyoto, he handed me a folded envelope. Inside was a sliver of washi paper with one word: *shizukesa*—quietude.

"When August comes, open it," he said. "Or not. Obon knows how to find you."

I have kept it unopened.

Back home, far from Japan, I wrote the names of those I missed on a square of paper and placed it beside a stick of incense. The wind stirred. That was enough.

One final fire
climbs the mountain's quiet back –
we bow to absence.

Author's Reflection

Why did I write about Obon without August? I was not there when lanterns touched the river. I did not join the Bon Odori circle. I did not watch the Daimonji blaze its farewell across Kyoto's sky.

But through Nobu—his stories, his silences, his pauses before memory—I received Obon like a folded letter from another life.

Some journeys are not taken on foot. Some months arrive even when you never turn the calendar page.

❄

❖ The Homing Dead

(Twin Echo to Obon: Where the Dead Return Gently Home)

Lanterns float downstream –
the river bends toward silence.
Footsteps without weight.

The lanterns came first before incense. Before chants. Before the quiet shuffle of slippers across tatami. Lanterns lined the narrow alleyways like fireflies tamed and tethered, casting their glow onto walls long accustomed to shadow. Kyoto's Obon did not begin with spectacle but with memory stitched into silence.

Sachiko Fujii returned every August not because she believed. Not entirely. At forty-three, a Tokyo-based software engineer who spent her days training predictive algorithms, her life was ruled by code, not ghosts. But Obon was different. Obon belonged to her family house in Nishijin, and in Nishijin, ghosts were not metaphors – they were inheritance.

Her brother Hiroshi, unmarried and rooted, lived there still. He kept the house like one tends an ageing parent: sweeping each room daily, sliding doors closed with reverence. On the altar: their father's smiling photo, their mother's stern one, a bottle of sake, and a pair of worn work shoes.

"Do you even light incense in Tokyo?" Hiroshi asked on her first night home.

Sachiko half-laughed. "I prefer deadlines."

He slid a cup of barley tea across the table. "Careful. Some of them watch even from the other side."

That night, the old house creaked as only ancient houses do—settling into the weight of its memories. She lay awake in her childhood room, watching the lantern outside paint trembling patterns on the shōji screen. And then she heard it: a soft thud, a sliding door, a brush of cloth on cloth.

She turned. Nothing. Only sandalwood in the air.

The next morning, their father's photo had shifted—angled now toward the kitchen.

"Did you move it?" she asked.

"Maybe he wanted breakfast," Hiroshi said.

They laughed. But the silence that followed remembered otherwise.

A lantern's drift on the second night, they joined the *tōrō nagashi,* floating lanterns, on the Kamo River.

Paper lanterns, each carrying an ancestor's name, were set afloat. The current gathered them gently, pulling them downstream like thoughts too heavy to hold.

Sachiko's hands trembled as she placed hers in the water. It drifted, then—impossibly—turned upstream. Just enough. Just once.

"It's the wind," Hiroshi offered. "Or the way you folded it."

But later that evening, their father's photo had tilted again—this time toward the engawa, where he used to sip beer and read paperbacks in the fading light.

The storm came on the third night. Rain lashed the tiled roof. Lanterns shivered in their hooks. Sachiko sat with her laptop open, pretending to work.

At 2:14 a.m.—the time of his recorded death—the lights flickered. The engawa door slid open.

Not violently. Gently. As if someone tired had returned from a long journey.

She rose, trembling. No one there. Only the faint scent of hops. And on the wooden boards, a dog-eared copy of *Shōgun* (the famous historical novel *Shōgun*—1975— by James Clavell; also a term for hereditary military dictator) lay open to page 72—the same page their father had always lingered on.

She lowered herself beside it.

"I missed your funeral," she whispered.

The rain softened. And in that moment, the whole house seemed to exhale.

On the final night, the mountains of Kyoto caught fire. Five vast bonfires—Daimonji, Myō, Hō, the boat, the torii—flared against the black sky, guiding spirits home.

Hiroshi stood beside her, the firelight reflected in his eyes.

"They say the dead leave quietly," he murmured. "No drama."

She nodded. "I think he just wanted to make sure we still remembered."

The next morning, the house was still. The photo was back in place. The Shōgun was gone. Only a faint ring-mark on the *engawa,* indoor verandah, remained, where a beer can once sat.

As the train pulled out of Kyoto Station, Sachiko watched the riverbanks blur with mist. In its shifting folds, she imagined a silhouette—faint, waving once, before dissolving back into fog.

Not haunting.
Just checking in.
Just… coming home.

❀

❖ Noh Theatre: Masks That Remember the Wind

Pine stage whispers low –
one mask tilts toward silence past
centuries of breath.

The Stage of Stillness

The theatre was nearly empty: a few elderly patrons, a French couple whispering, a schoolgirl with a sketchbook balanced on her knees. The lights were dim, not theatrical—more like twilight settling into wood.

There was no velvet curtain, no gilded proscenium, no prelude of music—only wood. Polished cypress, pale as bone, raised on stilts, roofed like a shrine. At its back, a single painted pine tree stood watch.

A Noh stage is less a place for performance than a vessel for time.

There is nothing but space.

And silence.

An Encounter Beneath the Pines

Before the play began, an older man in a pristine grey kimono leaned toward me. His face was weathered, his voice gentle.

"Is this your first Noh?"

"It is," I admitted. "I've heard it can be slow."

He chuckled softly. "Like the moon. Slow, but always arriving."

He introduced himself as Mr Yamamoto, a teacher of traditional music. His voice carried the ease of one accustomed to silence.

"Western theatre begins with plot," he said. "Noh begins with presence."

"Presence of what?"

"Of absence. Of longing. Of spirits not yet finished speaking."

Movement Slower Than Memory

The play, *Yamamba*—The Mountain Crone—began with a hush more potent than a fanfare. The shite, the principal actor, entered along the bridgeway, each step less motion than invocation.

His mask shimmered between states: sorrow, serenity, something uncanny. Not expressive in the Western sense, but suggestive—as if someone from another realm had brushed my shoulder.

Every gesture—raising a sleeve, tilting the head, placing a foot—was a calligraphy stroke drawn directly into air. The musicians' flute, drums, and voices spoke in gasps and wails: not accompaniment, but summoning.

"You don't watch Noh," Yamamoto whispered beside me.

"You wait for it."

Masks, Memory, and the Moonlit Path

During the break in performance, I lingered outside among paper lanterns swaying on wooden poles. A young performer, still streaked with white around his hairline, walked beside me.

"Your character was haunting," I said.

"She was haunted," he replied.

"By what?"

"By the part of herself that once lived. Noh isn't about ghosts. It's about remembering what we try to forget."

He glanced up at the moon.

"When I wear the mask, it sees me more than I see it."

The Sound of Things Not Said

For the final part, the play returned to *Atsumori*, the tale of a slain youth visited by his own grief. The ghost's mask tilted, the chant rose, and something in me shifted.

Not understanding—recognition. As if sorrow itself had crossed centuries to stand in the room.

My notes from that show were brief, only one line:

"Noh does not move forward. It descends."

The Teacher in Yamamoto

I caught up with Yamamoto-san as the crowd began to thin, steering him toward a nearby tea house and the comfort of a steaming bowl of matcha. For a foreigner, the move was bold, almost abrupt, and I offered a small bow of apology.

He regarded me with a wry kindness. "Ah, you are still uncertain about today's play, no?" A faint smile traced his lips as he lifted the cup. "Much of Japan resists quick understanding—Noh most of all."

I let the silence rest between us, meeting his eyes to show both contrition and intent.

"A Noh stage," he said at last, polishing the mist from his spectacles, "is less a place for performance than a vessel of time."

He lingered on the word *vessel*, letting it steep like the tea.

"A vessel is never merely passive. It holds, preserves, carries. So it is with Noh. Preservation—centuries of memory and ritual settle into those cedar boards like incense into wood. Transmission—each performance ferries the audience across eras, a ship on a quiet sea. And suspension—time gathers there, eddying in the pauses, unfolding outside the clocks we know."

What the Mask Leaves Behind

For weeks afterwards, I could not forget the mask. Not its face, but its echo — the way it mirrored mine when I was unguarded. The stage had not been theatre but shrine; the play, a prayer.

During our chat at the teahouse, I'd asked Yamamoto, "Why is Noh preserved so carefully?"

He did not answer at once. Then, quietly:

"Because it teaches us how to hold sorrow. Gently. Beautifully. Without rushing."

Final Curtain, Never Drawn

Now, when cicadas cry or moonlight falls across temple roofs, I think of that stage: the painted pine, the mask that did not express but allowed the world to enter.

Many arts dazzle, seduce, or argue.
Noh listens.
And in its listening, something eternal is heard.

❅

❖ Balancing Shinto and Zen

Petal in still stream –
a breath, not a declaration,
spirit walks unseen.

Arrival into Quiet

When I reached Japan in early May, the streets were scattered with the last cherry blossoms and the first shimmer of summer's green. Cities hummed with quiet precision, while forests—those vast cathedrals of cedar and pine—stood as if untouched by time. Something lingered in the air, between shrine stones and the hush of temple bells.

I came not only as a visitor, but as a seeker of stillness. Having been shaped by the layered, many-voiced spiritualities of India, I was curious: how does Japan, equally ancient, carry its faith?

The answer was not in sermons or scriptures. It was in the space between.

Where the Sacred Does Not Shout

To a visitor from the West—or from India—Japan's spirituality can seem elusive. There are no preachers on corners, no proclamations of creed. Shrines and temples appear without spectacle: tucked beside shopping arcades, emerging behind train stations, hidden in mountain folds.

And yet, for me, the rhythm was familiar. Like Hindu practice, Japan's faith resists the stark divide between believer and non-believer. It is not something one converts to; it is something one participates in.

Here, no declaration is required. One bows. One washes one's hands. One lets the sacred unfold at its own pace, unannounced.

The Twin Rivers

Japan's spirit flows through two streams running side by side: Shintō and Zen.

Shintō, ancient and indigenous, is a faith woven into nature. It reveres *kami*—spirits dwelling in rocks, rivers, winds, and ancestors. Shrines are less places of doctrine than encounters with season, presence, and the quiet fact of being alive.

Buddhism arrived later, in the 6th century, carrying sutras, rituals, and the path of liberation. But the two did not war. Instead, they folded together like silk layers in a kimono. Out of their meeting arose Zen—the austere radical. Zen stripped ornament from ritual, privileging silence, discipline, and direct experience: sweeping a floor as prayer, sitting until the self thins into awareness.

If Shintō sanctifies the world, Zen teaches you to step aside so you can see it.

Four Pillars of a Quiet Faith

❆ Reverence for Nature

In Shintō, nature is not a backdrop but a shrine. A twisted tree is not scenery; it is inhabited. A stream is not a symbol; it is a spirit. Reverence shows itself in small gestures: a gardener pruning a pine with seasonal care, a household placing a *kamidana* (god-shelf) above the stove. Nature here is never tamed—it is respected, sometimes feared, always seen.

❆ Impermanence

Zen does not turn from decay—it honours it. The falling cherry blossom is not a tragedy but a truth. This awareness—*mono no aware*—permeates poetry, gardens, architecture. Nothing is fixed, Zen reminds us. Not beauty. Not sorrow. Not even self. Fragility itself becomes meaning.

❄ Discipline and Introspection

In Japan, strength is quiet. You see it in the tea ceremony's exacting grace, in martial forms practised until they vanish into flow, in the silent bow of a railway attendant. Such gestures are not display but distillation: discipline as a mirror of inward clarity. In Zen, the monastery is not an escape from the world but a confrontation with it—without distraction, without noise.

❄ Spiritual Pragmatism

Perhaps most liberating is this: faith does not demand belief. Participation is enough. One may pray at a Shintō shrine before exams, hang an *ema* for love, toss coins at a Buddhist altar, and never once claim religion. This is not confusion but cultural wisdom: a spirituality designed not around dogma, but balance.

A Walk Through the Whisper

One morning in Kamakura, a forest trail opened onto a small Zen temple. It was not in any guidebook. No grand gate, no golden-robed monks—only the hush of bamboo and a wooden hall alive with presence.

I lingered as water dripped from a bamboo pipe into a stone basin: plunk, pause, plunk. The sound was a teaching in itself. There were no signs, no explanations—only an invitation.

So I bowed.

What the Silence Teaches

In Japan, I did not find a theology to explain. I found a posture to adopt. Not every sacred thing requires a name. Not every prayer needs words.

In a world restless for declarations, Japan offers a gentler gift: discretion. The sense that some truths are too subtle for slogans, too precious for certainty.

Like a haiku, its spirituality is spare, precise, resonant far beyond its lines.

Petal in still stream –
somewhere a god listens close
and does not reply.

❄

❖ The Seven Japanese Paths to the Summit

(Twin Echo to "Balancing Shintō and Zen")

Ikigai – The Gentle Pull of the Morning Bell

Where breath meets purpose,
and the plum tree in still bloom
outlasts the season.

There is an hour in Uji when even the wind holds its breath. It arrives just before dawn, as the shutters of the Yamamoto Tea Shop slide open without ceremony.

Nobu and I waited in the chill. He inclined his head toward the door.

"Daichi-san begins each day exactly so," he whispered. "The bell that wakes him is not a clock—it is the work itself."

Daichi Yamamoto, eighty-nine, tied the knot of his linen apron with the precision of a man who still believes in beginnings. The indigo cloth, softened by decades, carried his late wife's name stitched faintly into its hem—thread faded but enduring, like memory.

No music, no menu. Only porcelain cups, tea caddies, a broom, and a stillness in which even pause felt purposeful.

When I asked whether routine ever tired him, Daichi smiled.

"My body tires," he said softly, "my reason does not. This is not obligation. It is the bell that wakes me."

Nobu murmured, almost to himself, "Ikigai."

The steam carried the word into silence. A cicada shell clung to a tree. From the hills, a monk's bell rang—not a summons, but a release.

❄❄

Shikata ga nai – The Sea Cannot Be Held Back

Wind tears the kite string –
still, the boy keeps running,
as if it returns.

After the great 2011 Tōhoku tsunami had ripped through Sendai—flattening houses, swallowing fields, and leaving thousands homeless—relief shelters spread across the battered coast. Many now lived on government rations and the kindness of strangers, carrying memories that were heavier than the few belongings they'd saved.

In one of these temporary shelters, we met Sachiko Watanabe, arranging chipped bowls of rice and pickled daikon as if a banquet might appear. Her hands never rested: folding unworn clothes, wiping spotless tables, aligning spoons.

A young volunteer asked whether the work helped. She looked beyond him to a child's sandal abandoned in the gravel.

"My son flew kites," she said. "On the day of the wave, the wind snapped the string. But he kept running. As if it would return."

She poured tea, precise and weightless.

"Shikata ga nai," Nobu translated quietly. "It cannot be helped. Yet it helps us endure."

The sea could not be held back.
But rice could be warmed.
Radish shared.
Tea poured.
Enough to begin again.

❄❄❄

Wabi-Sabi – The Beauty of the Broken Bowl

Mended with gold dust,
the old cup on the table
holds both tea and time.

At a Kyoto flea market, I paused before a tea bowl stitched with gold, its fractures shining like veins of dawn.

Nobu lifted it gently.

"Kintsugi," he said. "Not to hide the break, but to honour it. A wound cared for becomes part of the whole."

That evening, we brewed tea in the bowl. The golden seam caught the lantern's glow like a scar turned toward sunrise.

"Not all damage diminishes," Nobu murmured. "Sometimes what returns is more complete."

❄❄❄❄

Gaman – Dignity in the Face of Fire

Snowstorm at the gate –
the lantern does not flicker,
only glows warmer.

At dawn in Akita, boys trained on a frozen baseball field, breath rising like steam. Their silence was unbroken.

"They don't complain," I said.

"Gaman," Nobu replied. "To endure without complaint. To prepare for what cannot be predicted."

Later, we watched a young girl bow again and again to her grandfather before boarding the train. He wept openly. Her eyes were wet, but her spine unbent.

Strength that absorbs pain—and still stands.

❄❄❄❄❄

Oubaitori – Blossoms Grow Differently

Four trees in full bloom –
each petal on its own time
still makes up the spring.

Under Nara's cherry trees, petals scattered like punctuation. Nobu brushed one from his sleeve.

"Tokyo taught me to compare," he said with a wry smile. "But the blossoms remind us: cherry, plum, peach, apricot—each blooms in its own season. No one asks which is best."

We raised cans of beer to the drifting petals.

"Oubaitori," he said. "Never compare. Bloom in your season."

❊❊❊❊❊❊

Kaizen - The Slow Spiral of Becoming

ain carves the mountain
not with rage or revolution –
only drop by drop.

In Tokushima, we visited Naoko Fujimura, stirring indigo cloth through a vat that darkened shade by shade.

"This scarf took twenty-three days," she said.

"Why longer next time?" I asked.

"Because I'm closer."

Nobu watched as the fabric slowly turned. "Kaizen," he explained. "No final version—only the courage to return again."

❊❊❊❊❊❊❊

Shu-Ha-Ri - To Know Is to Leave

The sparrow first learns
to fly by shadowing flight,
then forgets the sky.

In an Osaka rehearsal hall, a Noh master addressed his students:

"Shu. Ha. Ri. First obey. Then break. Then transcend."

Afterwards, Nobu said quietly, "Each art asks this of us. First learn, then depart. Only then can you create what is truly your own."

Epilogue – Lantern Light

Lanterns glowed along the Philosopher's Path like commas between breaths. Nobu and I walked without hurry, the canal holding a shimmer of moonlight.

We spoke little. The night already carried the seven truths: a cracked bowl, a scarf of indigo, a girl who bowed without breaking, an old man pouring tea, a woman who poured grief into rice.

Seven paths, seven lanterns—each flickering toward the same summit.

To learn is to imitate.
To understand is to stray.
To become is to forget—
and still remember.

Section III:

Memory, Resistance, and the Shadows of History

Where history resists erasure and memory hides in the folds of neon, silence, and soil, this section turns to Japan's shadows—those places where forgetting is impossible yet remembering is unbearable. Here lie the quiet rebellions of culture, grief, and art. In these pages, pachinko parlours hum with ghosts, monologues reveal what textbooks omit, and beauty itself becomes a battleground. War lingers not only in ruins, but in architecture, in ink, in film reels, in the restrained gaze of a nation still negotiating its past. For what is forgotten never truly disappears; it returns in altered shapes—in a masked performance, a silent protest, a single brushstroke of refusal.

Fire, Silence, and Renewal: A triptych

From the searing flash of *Hiroshima* to the quiet lament of *Japan, Don't Cry for Me,* and finally to the gentle insistence of *Ink, Not Blood,* this triptych of pieces traces a single arc of human resilience. Fire begins the story—sudden, merciless, and absolute. Silence follows, the stillness of grief where words falter and memory itself seems too heavy to bear. Yet out of that hush rises a different language: ink that records rather than wounds, gestures that heal rather than harm. Read together, these works affirm that devastation need not be the final chapter. What is shattered can seed compassion; what is lost can open space for unexpected light. In their company, we are reminded that a nation, like a soul, may be scarred but never extinguished—and that renewal often blooms most vividly where the world once burned.

Contents

11 Ghosts in the Pachinko Machine ★

12 Naoko's Monologue ★

13 Japan's Ancient to Modern History and Politics

14 Japan's Quiet Transformation

15 Japanese Films, Architecture, and Literature ★

16 Rento Rikitake Returns ★

17 Hiroshima ★

18 Japan, Don't Cry for Me ★

19 Ink, Not Blood ★

❖ The Ghost in the Pachinko Machine

Steel balls ricochet –
a silence behind the noise,
watching who forgets.

The Pachinko parlour was not on my itinerary.

I had mapped temples, cherry blossoms, hot springs, and even a teahouse chat on Noh theatre. But the neon-jagged cacophony of a Pachinko parlour felt, at best, an ambient backdrop to my otherwise graceful pilgrimage through "cultural Japan."

And yet.

Let me digress briefly to show how an unscripted detour can rival the best-laid plans.

I have a weak bladder. It's often a source of embarrassment, but it occasionally delivers comic detours into unexpected stories.

About a decade ago, in Washington, D.C., I was footloose and fancy-free, wandering the streets after my daughter dropped me off on her way to work. One day, stricken by my rebellious bladder in a downtown zone lined with sleek office blocks, I was desperate. The buildings looked forbidding – no public restrooms, no nearby cafés.

My daughter had warned me: "Don't try anything funny. You'll get fined. Or worse, deported."

It was September 2011. I had a thick beard and was carrying a backpack—enough, perhaps, to invite attention. Still, necessity won. I joined a stream of office workers entering a building. Security was tight—X-ray screening and burly guards—but to my surprise, they let me in after scanning my bag. I found the restroom. Bliss.

Emerging, I realised I had inadvertently entered a high-security corridor in the Hart Senate Office Building. Opposite the restroom door was Speaker Nancy Pelosi's office. I peeked in, and she was in the office. (Nancy Patricia Pelosi was the 52nd Speaker of the United States House of Representatives, serving from 2007 to 2011 and again from 2019 to 2023). With no scripted itinerary, I had time to kill. Emboldened, I took an impromptu, unescorted tour of the nine-storied upper floor and three-storied basement building—perhaps my life's most extended accidental civic engagement with the US Senate!

On this occasion, in Kyoto, my bladder once again betrayed me. This time, I ducked into a nondescript elevator and emerged on the top floor of a building filled with bright lights and hypnotic noise—rows and rows of blinking, kaleidoscopic machines—pachinko.

And so, the story truly begins.

Pachinko Galaxy 88

That morning, Kyoto's famed Philosopher's Path was overrun with tourists in rental kimonos and selfie sticks—modern-day samurai wielding filters. I veered off, like a raindrop refusing to follow the gutter.

I saw it somewhere between Gion's quiet alleys and a vending machine selling hot corn soup and chilled beer (Japan, you are a genius).

A glowing block of chrome and chaos.

Pachinko Galaxy 88.

Inside, the air was warm, recycled, and faintly metallic. Hundreds of tiny silver balls pinged through vertical labyrinths. The machines flashed like miniature Las Vegas shrines. I stepped cautiously out of the elevator, like one might step into a forgotten childhood arcade—or a temple.

I did not expect to meet a ghost.

Enter Kubo-san

"You don't strike me as a gambler," came a voice from behind.

I turned. An elderly man with Elvis Presley hair and a lavender bowling shirt gestured toward the empty machine beside him.

"I'm Kubo. Been playing here since the Showa era," he said casually.

"I don't even know how to play," I admitted.

He shrugged. "Nobody does. That's part of the charm. Sit—I'll teach you how to lose slowly."

So I sat.

The machine before me blinked seductively—cartoon cats danced between cherry blossom animations. A uniformed attendant handed me a tray of silver balls. Her bow-tied headband and serene politeness reminded me of someone trained to disarm bombs, not tourists.

"Turn this knob gently," Kubo instructed. "Like pouring sake into a very judgmental cup."

The balls sprayed forward.

Some bounced like puppies. Others dropped with quiet dignity into point slots that screamed with delight. Kubo's own machine suddenly burst into Beethoven, followed by a digital samurai yelling "YATTA!"

I jumped.

Kubo didn't flinch. "That's just the ghost," he said, deadpan.

I smiled. "You mean, the machine?"

He looked sideways. "No. The ghost. She lives in Machine #47."

Machine #47

He pointed across the aisle to a lone machine that stood slightly ajar. Unlike the others, it wasn't flashing. It was off, but still.

"Her name's Naoko. She used to work here. Played that machine every break—always the same rhythm. Like a heartbeat."

"What happened to her?" I asked, whispering for reasons I didn't understand.

"She passed away. But sometimes… that machine plays itself."

I waited for the wink, the laugh.

He didn't deliver.

Instead, he pulled a photo from his pocket: a woman with cropped hair holding a tray of Pachinko winnings, flashing a peace sign, her cheeks puffed mid-laughter, and a man with an unlit cigarette behind his ear.

"She said the machine whispered to her."

"What did it say?"

Kubo smiled slowly. "Keep playing. Don't go home yet."

Pachinko as Metaphor

There is something seductively absurd about Pachinko. It is loud yet private, meaningless yet ritualistic. The machines scream with every minor success, but no one claps or cheers. Everyone is alone, surrounded by a blinking chorus.

To a foreigner, it feels like a video game with no plot. To many Japanese, it's something else: a brief rebellion against structure, against relentless perfection.

"Sometimes I think Japan put its afterlife in these machines," I said.

Kubo grinned. "You think we worship ghosts in shrines only? No. They live here too. In noise. In plastic. In chance."

A silver ball rolled off my tray and onto the floor. I bent to pick it up—only to find a second one already there.

"Not mine," I said.

Kubo looked down. "Maybe hers."

Leaving the Parlour

I played for twenty more minutes, losing magnificently. I won nothing but the strange serenity of shared absurdity.

At the prize counter, Kubo insisted on getting me a small keychain shaped like a torii gate.

"For balance," he said. "Temples by day, Pachinko by night."

Before I stepped out into the Kyoto sunlight, ears ringing with phantom bells, I turned back.

Machine #47 was blinking now.

No one sat there.

Just the soft whirr of motion. One ball bouncing slowly, as if still deciding whether to fall or fly.

Author's Reflection

❄ In Japan, ghosts are generally considered benevolent. They are often melancholic, curious, and tender. They linger not for revenge but attachment—a leftover sigh of love.

I may have met one in that Pachinko parlour, among neon cats and synthesised chaos. Or at least, I met those who leave space for her return.

Now, wherever I go, I listen for stray rhythms in machines, the clink of dropped coins, or whispered instructions from unseen players.

Perhaps the divine doesn't speak in thunderclaps.

Perhaps it pings.

❄

❖ Naoko's Monologue

(Twin Echo to The Ghost in the Pachinko Machine)

Pachinko ghosts hum –
my name, lit in phantom code,
where no one looks up.

I shouldn't have gone back.

But Thursdays have a way of repeating themselves when grief forgets how to sleep.

The alley was still there—narrow, hesitant, the kind of place the city forgets to sweep. The ramen shop had folded into its own shadows. The cat, thinner now, limped with less ceremony, blinking at me as if to say: *You're late.*

The arcade's door sighed when I touched it.

Inside, time had peeled itself into layers:
the flicker of sodium lights,

the hum sounded like a throat clearing in another room,
the insomnia of machines.

And there it was.
Third row. Fifth from the wall.

Number Forty-Seven.

My machine.
His machine—gone these six months, unreported, as if the city itself forgot.

Our oracle—part slot machine, part shrine—where every click of steel moons felt like a question answered.

Its label long gone, only adhesive ghosts and rust shadows remained. But I would know that face in a crowd of a hundred thousand bells.

It pulsed.
It knew.

I pressed my palm against the glass. No heat. Only the cool breath of something that had forgotten how to die.

Once, I told myself it was superstition—that he could not haunt a contraption of ball bearings and LED nerves. But machines are patient. They do not argue. They wait for you to come back, broken enough to listen.

I touched the lever once, softly.

Steel moons settled in their orbit. The tray rattled with anticipation.

And then—
a pause.

His pause.
That exact, infuriating, reverent stillness before speaking, as though parsing silence for an omen.

I remembered the unlit cigarette tucked behind his ear—more promise than habit.

For a breathless moment, it flared in chrome.

A trick of light, they'd say.
But tricks are for the living.

This was a return.

Some say the dead speak in dreams.
Mine prefers circuitry.

I heard him inside the wiring—
not voice, but glitch,
a gentle stutter in the machine's breath:

"N…nao…ko?"

It spoke like a question,
like a spell misremembered.

Then the lights dimmed—just slightly—like someone leaning away.

I stayed until the hum collapsed into itself.
Until the balls stopped spinning.
Until the machine blinked one last, unsure eyelid.

When I turned to leave, the cat was waiting again. Still limping, but slower now. As though it, too, had heard something it could not explain.

Some nights I wonder—
Am I the ghost visiting the machine,
or is it the other way around?

In the mirror by my front door, I sometimes catch a flicker of someone pausing mid-sentence, a cigarette tucked behind his ear.

But the apartment is empty.
Always has been.

Machines do not mourn.
They wait.

And in their waiting, they teach something terrible:
Memory is not a possession.
It is a place.

And sometimes that place opens its door,
lets you in,
and locks it behind you.

Author's Reflection

❄ On Twin Echoes: On Ghosts and Forms

The Ghost in the Pachinko Machine and *Naoko's Monologue* were always meant as companions—two sides of the same invisible coin.

The former is essay: grounded, observed, haunted by allegory. The ghost is whispered, not seen—an echo of lives lost in repetition.

The latter belongs to fiction. Here, the ghost speaks. The machine breathes. The monologue gives shape to what memory alone cannot hold.

Together, they form a Twin Echo: one remembered by the living, the other whispered by the dead.

The essay remembers.
The fiction haunts.

❄

Japan's Ancient to Modern History and Politics

Footsteps on old stones –
time, law, tea, and breath entwine
in a quiet bow.

Beneath the Red Torii

Step off a train in Kyoto and the scent of incense greets you: pine, faint smoke, the hush of gravel paths. A vermilion torii frames the sky. Beyond it, silence hums with birdsong and the echo of clapping hands. A passerby bows deeply before crossing.

In Japan, time does not march—it folds. Rituals are not preserved as performance, but lived as continuity. To understand Japan is not to walk in a straight line but to spiral: circling through nature, history, and the soul.

Whispers in the Forest: Shintō Foundations

Before emperors or electronics, the people bowed to kami—spirits alive in waterfalls, cherry blossoms, or even in a grandmother's kitchen knife. This was Shintō: no scripture, no founder, no creed—only participation.

Even now, a businessman may pause at a roadside shrine before a meeting. Schoolchildren visit shrines for exam blessings. Matsuri festivals ignite towns with drums, lanterns, and ancestral reverence. Shintō does not insist on belief. It offers rhythm: cleanse, approach, bow twice, clap twice, bow again.

A Thousand-Year Spiral: Japan in Time

Japan's story is a long dialogue between upheaval and refinement, silence and spectacle:

- Nara Period (710–794): first permanent capital, rise of Buddhism, chronicles *Kojiki* and *Nihon Shoki*.
- Heian (794–1185): Kyoto's courtly bloom, the *Tale of Genji*, refined aesthetics.
- Kamakura (1185–1333): The first shogunate, the rise of samurai, the repelling of Mongols by *kamikaze*.
- Muromachi (1336–1573): Ashikaga rule, Noh theatre, tea ceremony, Zen gardens.
- Sengoku (1467–1615): Warring States chaos, Oda Nobunaga, Toyotomi Hideyoshi, firearms and Christianity arrive.
- Edo (1603–1868): Tokugawa peace, sakoku isolation, rigid hierarchies, flowering of haiku, ukiyo-e, kabuki.
- Meiji (1868–1912): fall of the samurai, Westernisation, rapid industrialisation, modern nation-state.
- Taishō (1912–1926): democracy's brief spring, artistic experiment, global tremors.
- Shōwa (1926–1989): militarism, WWII, atomic devastation, U.S. occupation, economic miracle.

- Heisei (1989–2019): economic stagnation, technological brilliance, natural disasters.
- Reiwa (2019–): demographic decline, cultural reassessment, pandemic-era resilience.

Stillness and Flow: The Arrival of Buddhism

In the 6th century, Buddhism arrived from Korea and China—bringing bronze Buddhas, sutras, and the philosophy of impermanence. Yet Japan did not discard its *kami*. Shrines and temples rose side by side: Shintō purifying, Buddhism consoling.

Zen later refined this dialogue. In raked gravel gardens, in tea prepared with unhurried precision, in the brushstroke of *sumi-e*, awakening was found not in doctrine but in silence, sword, or a perfect cup of tea.

Steel and Silence: Samurai Japan

From the 12th to 19th centuries, emperors reigned in name, but samurai ruled in deed. Bound by *Bushidō*—honour, loyalty, death before disgrace—they forged an age of discipline and restraint.

Under Tokugawa rule, Japan closed itself to the world. Peace endured for centuries, enforced by hierarchy and isolation. Yet within this stillness, art flourished: Noh theatre whispered through masks, calligraphy inked spirit into gesture, ikebana revealed the sacred geometry of flowers. Even today, one can still sense this hush in Japan's formality and harmony.

The Empire Awakens: Meiji Restoration

In 1868, the emperor returned to symbolic power. The shogunate dissolved. Railways cut through paddies. Western science, fashion, and armies arrived. But Japan absorbed rather than surrendered. Temples still stood. Kimonos fluttered beneath overcoats. Modernisation came not as erasure, but as adaptation.

Ashes and Apologies: War and Aftermath

The 20th century saw ambition turn catastrophic: empire, invasion, then ruin. Hiroshima and Nagasaki remain eternal warnings.

Under American occupation, Japan wrote a new constitution. Article 9 renounced war forever. This pacifist vow, though debated, still shapes the nation's conscience.

From Ruins to Robots: Postwar Japan

From rubble rose resilience. By the 1980s, Japan led in cars, cameras, and microchips—Walkmans in pockets, bullet trains on rails. Then the bubble burst. Stagnation settled, but not despair.

Even today, vending machines glow beside shrines, manga is bought before prayers, farmers bow as the Shinkansen streaks past. Old and new coexist—not as rivals, but as breath and body.

What Moves Japan?

Beneath its history run enduring values:

- Wa – harmony above self.
- Omotenashi – hospitality as quiet attentiveness.
- Giri and Ninjō – duty and feeling, always in tension.
- Wabi-sabi – beauty in imperfection, the chipped bowl, the fleeting blossom.

The Soul of Today's Japan

Religion is less confession than custom. Nearly all participate—few proclaim. Shintō blesses beginnings. Buddhism consoles endings. Christianity lingers in weddings and holidays. Many call themselves *mushūkyō*—non-religious—yet still bow at shrines or carry exam charms.

Faith here whispers. It inhabits gestures more than creeds.

A Nation of Contrasts: Politics and Pressures

Japan remains a constitutional monarchy. Emperor Naruhito is the 126th in a line tracing its mythic origins to the sun goddess

Amaterasu. The Liberal Democratic Party dominates politics, the guardians of continuity.

But pressures mount: an ageing population, vanishing villages, gender imbalances, precarious geopolitics. Japan answers not with bluster but with balance—adjusting, enduring, waiting.

Epilogue: When You're There

Reverence in Japan is quiet.

Bow rather than shake hands. Remove your shoes. On trains, observe silence. At shrines, cleanse your hands, clap twice, and let your presence itself be prayer.

Attend a summer festival, sip tea in a tatami room, sit still in a Zen garden. Watch how ancient and modern lean into each other, not colliding but coexisting—like mountain and mist.

Here, time does not march forward. It spirals upward, like incense smoke—past and present entwined.

And as the bamboo rustles and a temple bell echoes across the valley, you realise:

Japan does not explain itself.
It asks to be experienced.

❆

Japan's Quiet Transformation

mist curls on old stones –
silence speaks in shrine and train,
time bows to the wind.

First Sounds

The first sound I heard in Japan was not a voice, nor the scurry of tyres on wet Tokyo streets. It was the soft hiss of an automatic door at Haneda Airport.

It closed behind me not with finality but with grace—like a shōji sliding shut by an unseen hand. In that moment, I stepped into a world not bounded by geography but by sensibility.

What followed was not only travel across the island, but passage through centuries of aesthetic hush and cultural thunder. Japan does not shout. It murmurs. And to receive it, you must learn to listen.

Where Spirits Linger

At Meiji Jingu in Tokyo, I learned my first lesson.

The forest seemed composed of silence itself, as though each cedar was listening to something I could not yet hear. At a stone basin, an elderly woman showed me how to purify.

"Left hand," she whispered. "Then, right. The mouth. Do not drink."

Her sleeves brushed my wrist like dragonfly wings.

"You are washing the outer world from the inner one," she added.

That was the revelation: Shintō was not theology but choreography. It asked not for belief, but for acknowledgement—that the river, the mountain, even the wooden ladle carried *kami*, a sacred presence. Shrines sprout everywhere, from alleyways to cliff edges, not as spectacles but as reminders.

A Shrine Beside a Temple

In Osaka, at Namba Yasaka Shrine, a giant lion head gaped against the sky, guardian and stage in one. Around the corner, a small Buddhist temple hummed beside vending machines and a takoyaki stand.

I asked a priest whether Shintō and Buddhism ever conflicted.

He smiled as though I had asked if spring argued with autumn. "No," he said. "They take off their shoes at the same door."

Shintō honours presence. Buddhism contemplates impermanence. The lion roars; the sutra whispers. Together they form a koan: even neon cities carry old quiet, if you listen between things.

Nobu Nakamura's Lesson

It was my companion Nobu—interpreter, guide, and the gentlest man I knew—who deepened this lesson.

Walking with me past the stone lions of Osaka, he recalled a rainy season in Kanazawa's samurai quarter.

"The stones glistened like ink wash," he said. "Every tatami in a retainer's house lay so that no four corners touched. A caretaker told me: a samurai does not live at odds with his surroundings."

Nobu paused, folding his arms. "Bushidō isn't spectacle. It is alignment. The sword is sheathed as often as raised."

He spoke, too, of Tomoe Gozen, the female general, and of Saigō Takamori—the last samurai who led a doomed rebellion against rifles in 1877.

"Of course, he knew he would lose," Nobu said quietly. "It was never about victory. It was about not vanishing quietly."

Later, in Tokyo, he sometimes stood before Saigō's statue in Ueno Park, where the general is depicted with his dog. "Strange choice," Nobu said. "But perhaps the dog was the only one who never asked him to change."

Then he looked at me and added, "I go there when the city grows too fast. To remember there are ways to disappear with dignity."

He wasn't telling me history. He was teaching me how to carry it.

Continuity Through Restraint

From the samurai's code of *Bushidō* to the bowed head of a train conductor, Japan has long transformed constraint into continuity.

The Tokugawa era sealed the nation from the world for two and a half centuries. While Europe colonised, Japan refined: Noh theatre, tea ceremony, ikebana. Even today, when a tea master lifts a bamboo ladle as though it were the moon, the gesture feels eight centuries old—yet utterly present.

The Curtain Rises

The Meiji Restoration of 1868 shattered isolation. The samurai class fell, railways rose, Western suits mingled with the kimono. Japan did not erase its past. It adapted.

"Modernisation began with scissors," a student once told me, showing an 1872 clipping of a samurai protesting the loss of his topknot. And yet shrines remained, their incense curling beside new telegraph lines. Steel gears moved to the rhythm of old drums.

Shadows and Light

Japan's empire rose with ambition and fell in ashes. Hiroshima and Nagasaki remain not only tragedies, but warnings.

At the Atomic Dome, a volunteer told me:

"I am not here to accuse. I am here to remember. Because forgetting is the beginning of repetition."

Postwar Japan remade itself through restraint: its pacifist constitution, its resolve, its innovations in electronics and aesthetics. Hiroshima taught that survival itself could be a form of resistance.

Robots and Rituals

In Akihabara, a retired salaryman, now homebound, served me matcha through a telepresence robot. On his screen, he grinned. "The spirit lives—even in pixels."

At TeamLab, I walked barefoot across digital blossoms that bloomed and dissolved at my feet.

And yet, on New Year's morning, families still shuffled to shrines, bowing, clapping, bowing again—gestures older than their nation-state.

In Japan, robots and rituals coexist not as contradiction, but as continuation.

At a ryokan in Takayama, a hostess once knelt to serve me breakfast. I offered to serve myself.

"If I serve you," she replied softly, "I become full."

She meant it.

Author's Reflection

To walk in Japan is to leave your shoes at the door—not only of houses, but of assumptions.

Step softly. Let the land speak. You will not always understand. But if you bow—before shrines, people, and moments—you will feel.

A Kyoto priest once told me:

"You do not need to find God. You need to find quiet. That is enough."

Perhaps that is Japan's transformation: not its bullet trains or its neon, but its ability to teach that quiet is not absence. It is presence arranged with care.

Japan is not a destination. It is a meditation in motion. A theatre of the mind whose play begins when you stop trying to write the script.

❄

❖ Japanese Film, Architecture, and Literature

In film, home, and verse—
stillness braids the soul of things,
culture learns to bow.

Threshold

In a quiet Kyoto teahouse, you kneel on tatami. A pot breathes in the corner. The wall is plain, earthen; a fine crack runs through the plaster. It is not a flaw. It is the point.

Japan is stitched not by spectacle, but by what lives just beneath the surface: the melancholy of seasons, the brushstroke of restraint, the interval where sound falls away. What follows is a passage through cinema, architecture, and literature—guided by four soft, durable threads: wabi-sabi, yūgen, shibui, and mono no aware.

Cinema: Moving Stillness

Wabi-sabi — *The Twilight Samurai* (2002, Yōji Yamada)

A humble swordsman at history's frayed edge: a small house, mended clothes, undiminished dignity. Like a chipped tea bowl that warms the hand, the film honours the imperfect as the truest vessel of grace.

Yūgen – *Woman in the Dunes* (1964, Hiroshi Teshigahara)

Sand sifts without end; captivity becomes a meditation. Meaning is not declared but implied—mystery as atmosphere, the unseen as the film's deepest event.

Shibui – *Tokyo Story* (1953, Yasujirō Ozu)

Parents visit grown children; almost nothing "happens." Low camera angles, long silences, and corridors held in frame. Restraint becomes revelation—the quiet taste that lingers.

Mono no aware – *Only Yesterday* (1991, Isao Takahata)

A woman remembers as the train moves forward. The past cannot be grasped, only carried. Tenderness comes from the knowledge that everything passes—and is loved anyway.

Architecture: Space That Breathes

Wabi-sabi — Katsura Imperial Villa (Kyoto)

Weathered wood, curving paths, nothing glossy. The villa doesn't impress—it disappears into its landscape—beauty you earn by patience.

Yūgen — Ryōan-ji Rock Garden (Kyoto)

Fifteen stones in raked white. You can never see them all at once. Suggestion over statement; emptiness speaking louder than form.

Shibui — Ise Grand Shrine (Mie)

Rebuilt every twenty years, precisely as before. Unpainted wood, lucid lines, no ornament. Austere devotion made visible—simplicity matured into radiance.

Literature: Words as Fabric

Wabi-sabi — Kakuzō Okakura, *The Book of Tea*

An essay disguised as ceremony. The chipped bowl, the faded scroll, the fragrance of leaves—imperfection becomes instruction, and courtesy, a philosophy.

Yūgen — Murasaki Shikibu, *The Tale of Genji*

Moonlit corridors, falling petals, glances that speak more than speech. Desire is sketched in air; the unspoken holds the weight.

Shibui — Yasunari Kawabata, *Snow Country*

Winter prose, clean and cold. Nothing wasted, nothing resolved. Under each spare sentence, another sentence—unsaid.

Mono no aware — Haruki Murakami, *Norwegian Wood*

Memory drifts like leaves; love flickers, and grief arrives softly. A modern ache with an ancient pulse: what passes, shapes.

The Fabric Beneath

These are not genres so much as temperaments—ways of perceiving and arranging the world:

❄ Wabi-sabi teaches us to love the worn and mended.

❄ Yūgen invites us to feel what cannot be said.

❄ Shibui prefers restraint to display, depth to dazzle.

❄ Mono no aware honours the fleeting with tenderness, not despair.

Together, they form a cultural cloth—delicate, enduring—like threads that are almost invisible until they hold everything together.

Walk It, Feel It

When you bow at a shrine or lift a hand-formed cup, remember: these are not performances. They are echoes. Centuries of attention reside in the simplest gesture.

You are not merely observing Japan. You are stepping into its weave—
thread by thread, breath by breath—
until your stillness becomes part of its pattern.

❖ Rento Rikitake Returns Home

(Twin Echo to Japanese Film, Architecture, and Literature)

Ink on a white form –
the stamp of the lowliest clerk
can change the nation.

Rento Rikitake wore his tie too tightly knotted for a man whose job required so little voice. For fourteen years, he served as a clerk in Tokyo's Ministry of Agriculture – twelve of them indistinguishable. His life was like paper, in and stamped out – no policy, no debate, no consequence.

On the fifteenth anniversary of his employment, he did not report to his desk. Instead, he left his white shirt draped neatly over a chair, his ID card hanging from the doorknob, and boarded a local train out of the capital.

He returns to the soil. The rice fields of Kumamoto Prefecture received him like a son who had briefly forgotten his name. The air smelled of wet earth, miso broth, and memory. He took over an almost-abandoned patch of ancestral land, farming with hands softened by years of paperwork.

Villagers whispered at first: "That's Rikitake-san, the Tokyo man. Maybe he broke." But whispers faded when they saw he stayed. Through storms, failed harvests, and the quiet loneliness of dusk, he stayed.

He repaired irrigation channels. He helped mend the school roof. Every third Tuesday, he drove a widow to the clinic. There were no announcements—only presence.

When the Prime Minister visited on a campaign tour two years later, his motorcade became mired in a muddy lane. Rikitake, in worn boots and straw hat, pulled the lead car free with his farm tractor.

That evening, he was invited to the local office of the ruling party. He politely declined. Three invitations later, he relented.

His first speeches were in community halls—hesitant, halting, but honest. His voice carried no polish, but it burned with quiet anger at bureaucratic arrogance. Tokyo listened. Newspapers called him "The Farmer with the Fire."

In party meetings, he spoke little, but when he did, it was with the weight of someone who had once fled a life of empty memos. His critics called him unsophisticated. His supporters called him incorruptible.

When scandals fractured the party—a construction kickback, a minister's disgrace—they needed a compromise figure. Not too ambitious. Not too tainted. Someone the public could trust, but the factions could manage.

Rento Rikitake ticked every box.

He was sworn in as Prime Minister without slogan or landslide—just a bow. But control was an illusion. Within months, he restructured agricultural subsidies, blocked a mega-resort near a protected coastal village, and made unannounced visits to public hospitals. Reporters dubbed him *"The Reluctant Reformer."*

Asked in a televised interview how it felt to be Prime Minister, he said simply:

"Like being a clerk again. But this time, the paper I stamp affects lives."

Behind the curtain, factions grumbled. Letters circulated. Rumours whispered of accidents. He never flinched.

After four years in office, he returned to his home village and gave an unpublicised speech beneath a camphor tree. No media, only neighbours.

"I don't believe in revolution," he said softly.
"I believe in continuity—
with correction."

Then he stepped down. No memoirs, no gilded posts abroad. He returned to Kumamoto, to the same patch of soil.

One summer afternoon, a young reporter found him bending over the fields.

"Rikitake-san," she asked, "Do you regret leaving Tokyo the first time?"

He smiled, brushing dirt from his hands.
"That wasn't leaving," he said.
"That was arriving."

❋

❖ Hiroshima

(Triptych panel-I)

Ashes in the wind—
children's laughter rises still,
peace cranes take their flight.

The Hour the Sky Fell

At 8:15 a.m. on August 6, 1945, the sky above Hiroshima tore open. From that clear blue morning, death descended. The American B-29 *Enola Gay* released its 9,700-pound uranium bomb, cruelly named *Little Boy.*

In one blinding instant, light devoured shadow. A roaring wave followed, then silence. A mushroom cloud unfolded into the heavens while the city below dissolved into fire and ash. The world's first nuclear attack had begun—an ending disguised as a dawn.

A Walk Through Memory

Eight decades later, on 23 May 2025, I stood at "*baku-shin-chi,*"—ground zero, hypocentre— which refers to the point on the Earth's surface directly below an airborne explosion of the atomic bomb dropped on Hiroshima, which exploded in the air.

The Hiroshima Peace Memorial Park lay before me—solemn, green, impossibly still. Within it: the museum, the Cenotaph, the Children's Peace Monument, the Atomic Dome.

At the stone cenotaph, I bowed not only for the 140,000 whose lives vanished in fire, but for the soul of humanity itself. The air, though calm, felt dense with memory.

In my schoolbook, Hiroshima had been a date, a statistic, an examination fact. Here, it was a whisper of uniforms never worn again, laundry never folded, shutters never opened. Ghosts of ordinary lives, interrupted mid-gesture, still pressed upon the air.

The Museum's Wordless Cry

The Peace Memorial Museum does not whisper.

It screams in a silence that scalds.

Textbooks become lies the moment you step inside.

On the walls: shadows seared into stone—the negative copy of a vanished world.

Watches forever frozen at 8:15, the instant time itself broke.

A child's tricycle, buckled and black, wheels fused like melted bone.

Outside, the rivers once bore no blossoms.

They carried bodies, hundreds, their reflections trembling in water the colour of ash.

Survivors staggered through a daylight darker than night:
skin peeling in long ribbons,
mouths coughing black smoke,
tongues charred to cinders and still pleading for water.
Eyes glowed red as furnace coals,
lips burned away to show teeth chattering in naked skulls.
Breath clawed at air that would not forgive.
Here, morality was not merely tested — it was vaporised.
No myth. No distance.
Only the unbearable fact of human flesh unmade.

Conversations with the Past

An elderly volunteer awaited me—a hibakusha, one who had walked through fire and kept breathing.

Her hands trembled, not from age alone, but from memories that still burned.

She led me to a tree whose bark was furrowed with black scars, each groove a vein of remembered flame.

"It was a sapling then," she said, her voice thin as smoke. "Burned... but alive. Like us."

I asked how a city of ash could rise again.

She let the question hang, the silence heavy as the summer heat that once turned flesh to mist.

Finally, she spoke—softly, but with the weight of a funeral bell.

"We had no choice," she said. "The dead could not speak. So we became their voice—every breath we take, a testimony carved from fire."

Her eyes held the shimmer of molten glass,

a vow forged in a morning when the sun fell to earth.

The Children's Noiseless Scream

At two years old, Sadako Sasaki outlived the white-hot flash that erased a city.

Ten years later, the hidden fire inside her blood began its slow, merciless bloom.

As her strength thinned to a whisper, she turned to an old legend:

a thousand paper cranes might summon healing, might bargain with the gods.

Her fingers—thin as the paper itself—creased and folded,

each crisp edge a quiet defiance,

each fragile wing a vow that life could rise from cinders.

She died before her thirteenth birthday,

but her cranes escaped the hospital walls,

bright fragments of resistance that now drift far beyond Hiroshima's Peace Park—

tiny messengers of hope stronger than war.

I stand at the Children's Peace Monument.

Schoolchildren kneel in a hush broken only by the rustle of coloured paper.

Their small hands flicker like birds in flight,

fold after fold, a thousand tiny hearts learning how to remember.

"Why do we fold them?" a teacher asks.

"To remember Sadako," a child answers, voice barely louder than the breeze.

Their chorus rises—a breath, a prayer—
not just mourning, but an unbroken promise
that the smallest hands will keep shaping peace
long after the last echo of the bomb has faded.

Reflections in the Present

Standing in Hiroshima, the headlines of today bled through the quiet:
tanks grinding across European fields,
missiles arcing over Asian skies,
nuclear threats tossed like casual dice.
Gaza. Ukraine. India. Pakistan.
The same worn vocabulary—*existential threat, red line, unprovoked aggression*—
words that once promised "Never Again" and now echo Again and Again.

The mushroom cloud has not vanished.
It lingers—not above the city, but inside our politics,
curled in the dark silos of stockpiled warheads,
drifting through the soft fog of our dangerous forgetfulness.

A City Reborn

And yet Hiroshima breathes.
It has rebuilt without erasure,
laying new bridges across rivers that once carried fire.
Students fill lecture halls where rubble once smouldered.
Baseball cheers ripple through a sky that once burned white.
The city carries memory like a heartbeat—steady, unhidden.

As I turned to leave, a cluster of schoolchildren gathered beneath Sadako's statue,
their song rising brighter than the thousand paper cranes they offered,
an octave of hope cutting clean through the centuries of ash.

The Final Bow

I knelt and placed a white chrysanthemum beneath the cenotaph.
The flower looked small, almost weightless, against the enormity of stone and silence.
Yet to bow was to refuse amnesia.
Silence, I understood, can be complicity;
memory is its own act of resistance.

Hiroshima does not ask for tears alone.
It demands witness.
It asks us to listen, to speak, to remember with courage—
and to guard the living from ever becoming such ghosts again.

Author's Reflection

❄ Why Language Matters

There are moments when numbers turn to ash and dates ring hollow.

Hiroshima is one of them.

To write *"the heat of the blast"* may be accurate.
To write *"the burning heart of the blast"* returns the human cost to words—
it lets language bleed.

A child's tricycle, melted into a black coil of grief, tells more truth than a thousand casualty charts.
A single shadow fused to stone is a moral argument no statistic can silence.

Emotion is not indulgence.
It is memory's last defence.
When history falters, language must carry the weight of the unspeakable,
its syllables glowing like coals in the dark.

The Trees That Survived

Four ginkgo trees once stood near the hypocentre.
They burned. They blackened. They were stripped to bone.
And yet, when the next spring unfurled,
green shoots pierced the scorched bark.

Today they still stand, leaves shimmering like quiet flames.
In Japanese art, the ginkgo symbolises endurance, longevity, and tranquil beauty.
In Hiroshima, they are not symbols.
They are witnesses that refused to die.

Epitaph for Hiroshima

May the souls of Hiroshima rest in peace.
May the living prove worthy of their memory.

❄

❖ Japan, Don't Cry for Me

(Triptych II)

Ashes in silence –
even in bloom, some cities
cry without a sound.

It begins with silence.

Not reverence, not peace—something halted mid-breath, a pause so deep the cicadas choke on it.

Twelve-year-old Ichiro Ichikawa feels the hush before he feels the heat.

Hiroshima summers are always hot, but never this still.

His mother, Hiraki, and little sister, Kimiko, are boiling barley tea when the sky ignites.

No siren. No warning. Only a flash so white it erases colour, then a brightness beyond light—an absence that devours.

The world folds in on itself.

He runs—or thinks he runs. Little Kimiko is startled, spilling the boiling tea on her face. The single red ribbon in her hair turning black.

Fragments remain: a woman with no face stumbling through smoke, a steel gate crumpling like paper, his mother's hand clamping his for one heartbeat—then gone.

The next clear memory is months later in Kyoto, at a distant relative's house.

They call him *lucky*.

The word tastes of iron.

He does not speak for days, only draws circles, shadows, a little boy with one shoe.

Half a century passes.

Ichiro is a janitor in a junior high school west of Tokyo, wearing quiet like a second uniform.

No one knows.

Not the headmaster.

Not the teachers.

Not the curious girl from class 2-B who helps him sweep the music room each Thursday.

"Ichikawa-san," she asks one afternoon, "why don't you ever play the piano?"

He shrugs. "My music days are over."

"But you hum," she says. "Always the same tune."

He hadn't noticed.

It is a lullaby—his mother's lullaby—carried intact across a ruined half-century.

On the morning of August 6, a letter arrives from the Hiroshima Peace Memorial Museum.

They have found a sketch: a boy with one shoe, a single tear streaking down an ash-stained face, signed *Ichiro I.*

He had forgotten sending it.

They ask him to come. To speak.

He hesitates.

The last time he tried, as a teenager, no one believed him.

But he boards the Shinkansen.

Hiroshima greets him with shiny glass and neon, buses calling stops in English, vending machines blinking friendly blue.

Yet beneath the bustle, the old silence seeps up through the soil.

He walks past the river, past the skeletal Dome.

Ghosts rise from the ground like people late for an appointment.

Inside the Memorial, a young guide bows, reciting practised facts.

He pins a badge on Ichiro's chest: *Atomic Bomb Survivor – Hibakusha.*

Ichiro touches it as though it might crumble.

Children wait—mostly twelve years old, his age when the sun fell to earth.

Some bored, some curious.

One boy, restless, looks uncannily like him.

"Ichiro-san," a teacher prompts, "would you like to begin?"

He steps forward.

But he does not speak.

He hums.

The lullaby threads the air, thin but unbroken, a sound that carries what words cannot bear.

The room stills: the fidgeters, the whisperers, all of them listening because the hum holds the memory of fire.

"I was twelve," he says at last.

"Unlike many others, I survived. My mother did not. My city changed. So did I. But the tune remained."

He unfolds the paper sketch and lifts it high.

"No matter how many buildings we raise, some memories need space. Not to wound us. To remind us."

He steps back.

No applause.

Only breath.

That night, in his narrow Tokyo apartment, he lights a stick of incense, sets out a bowl of rice and a cup of tea.

He whispers, "Tadaima." *I'm home.*

The air shifts—

not wind, not ghost—

something gentler.

A presence,

as if someone is listening.

Hiraki and Kimiko Ichika's August Sixth After-hours Watch

Every August sixth, the city remembers.

The air along the Motoyasu River thickens with incense and the sound of sandals on stone, but at midnight the park empties.

Only the bronze Dome remains—ribcage of a building, breathing moonlight.

I come when the crowds have gone, though I never plan to.

The clock drags me here like tide.

Tonight, the river is a mirror of black glass.

Lanterns from the day's memorial drift downstream, their small flames unsteady.

I kneel to release one of my own, but the water folds open before I touch it.

From the widening dark rise figures of lightless rain.

Men and women, children, the quick and the unburied, emerging as if the river remembers every name.

They are not transparent; they are *too* real—skin pale as salt, eyes full of unwritten histories.

One child steps forward, a girl with a single red ribbon in her hair. A deep-burn scar runs across her stoic face.

Her mouth moves without sound, yet I hear her clearly inside my chest:

"Don't flinch."

The lanterns around us flare.

Shadows blossom upward, forming streets I have never walked:

a marketplace where paper cranes fall like snow,

a tram whose windows hold the reflection of a sun that never rose again,

a house filled with clocks all stopped at 8:15.

The girl leads me through this shifting city.

Every doorway we pass releases a different scent—miso soup, scorched iron, the soft sweetness of persimmons long out of season.

She pauses before a bridge that glows as if made of moonlit bone.

"This is where the world split," she whispers.

A bell tolls beneath the river, low and endless.

The girl opens her hand.

Inside rests a single grain of black sand, pulsing like a heartbeat.

"When the last witness forgets," she says,

"this becomes a star. And falls again."

The bridge dissolves.

The city folds back into water.

The ghosts step into their own reflections and vanish, leaving only the lanterns, each flame suddenly bright enough to rival the moon.

I wake at dawn on a park bench, the river calm, my own lantern floating far downstream.

In my pocket is the grain of black sand, still warm.

When I close my hand around it, I hear the bell again –

not an echo, but a promise

that memory, if held tightly enough,

can burn longer than fire.

Meanwhile, outside Ichiro Ichikawa's narrow Tokyo apartment, day breaks, the bowl of rice is empty of the last grain. The tea is taken.

The stick of incense still glows brightly against the blue-grey smoke curling into memory.

❄

❖ Ink, Not Blood

(Triptych III)

River carries light –
names inked into falling ash,
no footsteps return.

Hiroshima, 1951.

The city stirs with cranes and scaffolds, but Hiroto Hamamoto does not rebuild.

Each day, he wanders the ruins like a man lost between calendars, a ghost adrift in his own body.

Once a professor of classical literature, now mute and hollow, he lives alone in a single narrow room beside the Motoyasu River.

The flash had taken everything – his wife Aiko, their children Kazuo and little Emiko –

no goodbyes, no bodies, only the silence of vapour.

Words, his lifelong companions, had betrayed him.

He survived, but survival felt like the cruellest death.

One rain-heavy morning, a scent arrests him mid-step: camphor wood, raw sumi ink, a fragrance older than grief itself.

Behind a half-rebuilt torii glows a thin shaft of lantern light.

A small shop bears a weathered sign: *The Soul of Writing*.

"Please enter," calls a voice from behind the noren curtain. "Even silence has a name."

Hideo Sato emerges—fingers callused, indigo robe damp from the rain, a stillness about him as if he has outlived fire itself.

"You breathe," he tells Hiroto, "but you do not exhale."

Hiroto bows, bones remembering a life before ash.

"No words," Sato says. "We begin with the hands."

Weeks pass. Hiroto returns in silence, watching Sato grind ink in slow, deliberate circles, the sound like distant rain on stone.

"Why not use bottled ink?" Hiroto asks at last.

Sato smiles. "Because that is liquid surrender."

He dips a brush, a single black stroke blooming across the paper.

"This," he says, "is resistance."

"Against what?"

"Against forgetting. Against despair."

One grey afternoon, Sato unfurls a scroll marked with a single character: —*mu*, emptiness.

"Zen monks spend lifetimes with this word," he says. "What do you see?"

Hiroto studies the stroke. "A tree that grew in silence, then fell unheard."

Sato's eyes glint. "Closer than most."

That night, Hiroto dreams of ink bleeding into paper, forming the names he has not spoken in six years.

At dawn, he returns, dips the brush, and writes: —*inochi*, life.

The character trembles. But it stands.

For the first time since the blast, so does he.

Seasons wheel. One autumn evening, Sato offers him a poem by Ono no Komachi:

Colour of the flower
has already faded away,
while in idle thoughts
my life passes vainly by,
as I watch the long rains fall.

"The brush remembers who we were," Sato murmurs.

That night, Hiroto begins a letter—not to officials, not to history, but to Aiko, Kazuo, Emiko.

Six years of silence spill across the page: regret, memory, love.

At dawn, he folds the paper and sets a match to it.

The ash spirals upward, a thin grey echo of the morning they left.

"Forgive me," he whispers to the smoke.

In the dream that follows, they return.

Aiko, hair loose as in younger days, smiling.

Kazuo with his father's crooked grin.

Emiko, laughing barefoot through silver grass.

They come without reproach, carrying only peace.

"We felt nothing," Aiko says softly. "It was over before we knew."

"Like falling into a warm dream," Kazuo adds.

Emiko twirls, her voice a bell: "We're happy."

Aiko cups his cheek. "Let go of the fire, Hiroto. You no longer carry it. Only love remains."

He wakes at sunrise. A single tear slides down his face. It no longer burns.

He returns to the shop. The inkstone waits, the brushes ready.

This time he writes: —*ki*, to remember.

Then: —*shin*, forgiveness.

Sato nods. "Your hand has caught up to your heart."

Years pass. Sato dies quietly, brush still wet in his grasp.

Hiroto inherits the studio. He never advertises, never signs his scrolls.

Children call him *the man who writes whispers*.

Tourists sit in reverent silence, watching black ink bloom into living silence.

Every August sixth, he walks to the riverbank.

On a sheet of rice paper, he writes a single word— *ai*, love—and lets it drift downstream.

The current carries it toward the sea, the strokes dark and luminous until water turns them to sky.

In Hiroshima, the soul of resistance is not in slogans but in brushstrokes.

When blood dries, ink flows.

When pain fades, memory remains.

And sometimes, if we are very quiet, the ones we lost return—

not to haunt,

but to heal.

Ink, not blood. Always.

❄

Rinno-Ji Buddhist Temple, Tochigi Prefecture, Japan

Bon Odori, the communal dance

Vegetarian Temple Cuisine

Piss Alley's Meat and Fish Grill

Traditional Hand-pulled Rickshaw

Cultural Reign of Cats

Gothic Lolita / Cosplay

Yakuza

Household Kamidana—God-shelf

Inside Buddha Temple

Section IV:

Creatures of Sign and Whimsy

Where meaning wears a whisker or a grin, this section follows the creatures and curiosities that animate Japan's cultural imagination. Here, cats are never merely pets—they are talismans, empresses, and keepers of quiet authority. Toys, too, are more than childhood diversions; they are storytellers, tricksters, and sometimes mirrors, reflecting both delight and unease. In this realm, whimsy is never shallow. A beckoning paw, a painted mask, a spinning top—each gesture conceals an older logic, each form is steeped in sign and spirit. To enter is to discover how the playful and the profound, the mischievous and the mysterious, sit side by side comfortably in Japan's living culture.

Contents

20 The Cultural Reign of Cats

21 A Tale of Two Tails and Two Royalties

22 The Enigmatic Japanese Toy

The Cultural Reign of the Cat

Silken tail flicks once –
on temple steps, a cat waits.
Even gods pause here.

Somewhere between a yawn and a tail flick, the cat quietly conquered the world—and we only noticed after surrendering.

The revelation didn't come to me through social media spirals or midnight cat videos. It arrived in the most unlikely of sanctuaries: the Hiroshima Museum of Art, in a gallery bathed in the mellow light of summer. I had gone seeking reflection, perhaps solace. Instead, I stumbled into a feline dominion.

Wall after wall, frame after frame: cats presiding over domestic interiors, cats curling into courtesans' sleeves, cats crouched like miniature gods at the feet of geisha, cats leaping mid-air into eternal play. They were not props, not ornaments. They were participants—present, poised, decisive. In those brushstrokes, I saw not companionship, but quiet sovereignty.

Dogs may be man's best friend—loyal, eager, bound by duty. But cats? They are arbiters. Observers. Judges with whiskered patience. They do not fetch. They do not obey. They do not beg. Instead, they gaze at us with detached amusement, minor deities toying with our devotion. Perhaps this is why we elevate them—not despite their aloofness, but because of it.

The Old Gods Had Whiskers

To trace their reign, one must step back—far back—to the Egyptian sands. Bastet, goddess with the feline head, reigned not as mascot but as sentinel of hearth and womb, guardian of music and fertility. To harm a cat was to court execution. Households shaved their eyebrows in mourning. Beloved cats were mummified, wrapped in linen so they might prowl eternally beside their masters.

India, too, knew the cat's sanctity. To kill one—even by accident—was to risk damnation. Atonement demanded a golden cat, full-sized and weighty as the departed. A fat tabby, then, could bankrupt a king. The old gods, it seems, wore whiskers and demanded tribute in purrs or precious metal.

Across deserts and continents, one truth stretched like a cat in the sun: wherever humanity sought mystery or solace, there too crouched a feline, unimpressed and immortal.

Nine Lives in Ukiyo-e

Centuries later, in Japan's Edo period, cats inked themselves into ukiyo-e woodblock prints. Courtesans, poised in layers of silk, shared their chambers with soft-pawed companions. Each curled tail, each watchful eye softened the formality, adding intimacy—and perhaps defiance—to the scene.

Folklore gave them deeper shadows. The bakeneko, the shapeshifting ghost-cat, prowled in whispers and nightmares. Its gentler descendant, the maneki-neko, now raises a paw from every shopfront in Japan, beckoning luck and prosperity. Myth or charm, trickster or guardian—cats embodied both. They still do.

Europe and the Feline Pendulum

In Europe, cats endured a darker arc. In the Middle Ages, they were branded demonic accomplices, hunted alongside women accused of witchcraft. Yet the Renaissance reclaimed them. Leonardo da Vinci himself declared, *"The smallest feline is a masterpiece."* One imagines him saying so while a cat, unimpressed, toppled his inkpot.

The pendulum swung—but the cat endured, always.

The Meme and the Muse

Today, they reign in two worlds: as luxury icons and digital monarchs. From Karl Lagerfeld's cosseted Choupette, complete with staff and inheritance, to the immortalised memes of Grumpy Cat, Lil Bub, and Nyan Cat streaking endlessly across screens, cats are everywhere. Their sovereignty stretches across galleries, billboards, hashtags, and hearths.

Why? Because they embody contradiction. They are soft and sharp, aloof and affectionate, wild and domestic. They mirror the freedom we crave: unapologetic selfhood, impervious to approval. They are myth in motion—modern muses wrapped in fur.

Portraits with a Tail

Back in Hiroshima's gallery, I realised the art was never solely about the cats. It was about people with cats—their touch, their trust, their shared silence. The cats were punctuation: a comma softening formality, an ellipsis deepening mystery, an exclamation mark curled into a question.

Epilogue with Whiskers

So yes—between a yawn and a flick of the tail, cats conquered us, not with force, but with stillness. Their dominion is not loud, but languid—stretching across sunbeams, watching through half-closed eyes, reminding us that sometimes sovereignty is silent.

We do not own cats. We orbit them. We mythologise them, meme them, paint them into eternity. Their reign is not conquest, but cohabitation. And that Mona Lisa smile we puzzle over? Perhaps, after all, it was the cat's idea.

A Tale of Two Tails and Two Royalties

Soft paws cross court floors –
one bows in silk reverence,
one barks through the fog.

Between the silken hush of Kyoto's chambers and the tartan-draped fields of Balmoral stretches an unlikely lineage of diplomacy: the dog. Not the battlefield hound or the farmhand shepherd, but the companion—courtier in fur, emissary of affection.

This is the story of two such creatures: one born of imperial Japan, the other of pastoral Wales. By accident or design, the Japanese Chin and the Pembroke Welsh Corgi rose to prominence not through conquest but charisma. In their bearing, they reflected the empires they served—mirrors of their monarchs, and through them, of their nations.

The Chin Who Bowed Before the Throne

In Edo's palaces—where poems drifted like incense and bamboo groves exhaled their sighs—the Japanese Chin appeared not as a pet but as a presence. With hauntingly human eyes and dainty, deliberate steps, the Chin seemed choreographed by the same invisible hand that guided the tea ceremony.

Its origins are debated: perhaps borne across the sea by a Korean envoy, possibly gifted by Chinese monks, or perhaps carried in the sleeve of a pilgrim. Wherever it came from, it arrived not to guard, herd, or fetch—but to witness.

Its tail curled like calligraphy. Its silence radiated more eloquence than bark. It was more *ukiyo-e* (refers to the woodblock prints and paintings during the Edo period—1603-1868) than utility, a porcelain creature that blurred the line between ornament and oracle. In the imperial court, the Chin was not taught tricks. It listened to poetry, lingered at the hems of emperors, and embodied a presence of ritual dignity.

Through the Chin, Japan's ceremonial self was revealed: hierarchical, refined, introspective—an empire that sanctified stillness.

The Corgi Who Charmed a Queen

Across seas and centuries, in the damp fields of Wales, the Pembroke Welsh Corgi began not in courts but in cow pastures. Legend says they were steeds of fairies—enchanted dogs saddled by woodland sprites. More pragmatically, they were low-slung herders, sharp of bark, bold of bite, keeping cattle in line with fearless nips at their heels.

Enter Princess Elizabeth.

Her first Corgi, *Susan*, became the ancestor of a royal line that bounded through Buckingham's halls for over seventy years. Where the Chin whispered grace, the Corgi yapped with irreverent charm.

These dogs were companions, jesters, and guardians of the Queen's private world. They appeared in photographs, barked at dignitaries without ceremony, and tumbled along the corridors of Windsor. Short-legged and audacious, the Corgi embodied a monarchy shifting from empire to emblem—its authority softened by affection, its continuity marked by wagging tails.

The Chin carried silence.

The Corgi carried laughter.

Both commanded attention.

Reflections in Fur

At first glance, they could not be more different.

One is porcelain; the other, pint-sized thunder.

One thrives on decorum; the other on disruption.

And yet, both became cultural emissaries.

The Chin evoked Japan's old gravitas: ritual, hierarchy, and the poetry of the unspoken. The Corgi embodied Britain's resilience: cheerful, unbothered, mischievous, and loyal. Neither was merely a pet. Each became a metaphor in motion—a living symbol of how empires present themselves to the world.

Monarchies are often called relics, outdated rituals clashing with modernity. But in these two breeds we glimpse something more intimate than crowns or sceptres: the human desire for companionship that softens power. The Chin was a confidant of silence. The Corgi, a jester of joy. Both curled beside rulers as custodians of memory.

Enduring Paw Prints

Today, the Chin is more likely to be seen on Park Avenue than in Kyoto's courts. The Corgi, though its royal spotlight dimmed with the Queen's passing, thrives in memes and merchandise—on tea towels, postage stamps, and Instagram reels.

Their legacies persist not through bloodlines but through stories. We remember the Chin's stillness in an age of noise. We recall the Corgi's exuberance in corridors of power. One teaches presence. The other teaches play.

Perhaps, as thrones falter and empires fade into footnotes, what endures are not rulers but the creatures who padded beside them.

The Last Bow, the Final Bark

To walk through history with animals is to humanise its heights and soften its blows.

The Chin bowed—teaching that dignity needs no words.

The Corgi barked—proving that mischief, too, can be regal.

Two tails, two empires.

Not rivals, but a duet.

Soft. Alert. Watching. Waiting. Remembering.

❄

The Enigmatic Japanese Toy

Soft thread, stitched in hush –
a country breathes through cloth,
dreams cupped in small palms.

When I landed in Tokyo in the summer of 2025, I carried a pocketful of assumptions. I expected precision: the sterile swoosh of bullet trains, vending machines aligned like obedient soldiers, the sacred hush of subway cars. I found all of that. Tokyo revealed itself in paradox—neon towers climbing beside moss-grown shrines, cafés staffed by robots, a street away from weathered temples watched by foxes.

And yet what disarmed me was not spectacle, but something smaller. Almost invisible.

A Toy.

Not a mascot. Not an anime character. Not an advertisement.

Just… a Toy. Unnamed, ubiquitous, and strangely resonant.

The First Sighting

It began as a glimpse: peeking from the pocket of a schoolgirl's backpack in Shibuya. Soft, round, with stubby arms and stitched eyes like two half-moons, its mouth an unreadable line—neither smile nor frown, but something in between.

Ten minutes later, I saw it again—dangling from the briefcase of a suited man at Shimbashi Station—a corporate soldier carrying the same silent talisman.

By lunchtime, the sightings multiplied, propped beside a ladle in a ramen shop in Ebisu. Resting beside incense and fruit in a Kyoto temple. Even faintly tattooed on the ankle of a boy stretched out in Yoyogi Park, headphones leaking lo-fi beats into the dusk.

What was this thing?

Questions in Translation

In Kyoto, beneath a wisteria canopy outside a stationery shop, I asked an elderly man sweeping his tiled entrance.

"Sumimasen," I said, pointing to the embroidered figure on his apron. "What is this?"

He looked down as though noticing it for the first time.

"Ah," he murmured, smiling faintly. "*Kokoro no fuku* – blessing for the heart."

He said no more. The broom resumed its quiet rhythm, as if the answer itself were sufficient. Perhaps it was.

Fragments of a Whole

In the days that followed, I collected fragments. Not explanations – glimpses.

At a station near Fushimi Inari, a mother whispered, her child asleep on her shoulder:

"My daughter says the Toy listens to her dreams. The good ones, it keeps. The frightening ones, it eats."

In Osaka, a language student confided:

"I've had mine since I was six. It's like… a soul's barcode. You don't scan it. It scans you."

At a riverside shrine in Arashiyama, a monk with parchment robes said softly:

"Some spirits are too quiet for names. The Toy is a vessel. It carries your unseen weight."

Public, Yet Private

What struck me most was how publicly private it remained. The Toy was everywhere—stitched, pinned, inked—yet no one remarked on it. Unlike Western mascots, loud and transactional, it sold nothing. It jingled no slogans. It simply accompanied. Like breath. Or memory.

A Thought at Dusk

On a bench along Kyoto's Philosopher's Path, cherry blossoms drifted into the Kamo River like forgotten syllables. Two teenagers passed. One with the Toy swinging from his belt. The other was with it stitched into her sleeve, nearly hidden.

And suddenly I thought: we all carry something. Visible or unseen. The Toy was theirs.

Phones announce power.

Watches, time.

Cars, success.

But the Toy whispers: *I am tender. I am trying. I remember what hurt, and what healed.*

A Conversation in Gion

In Gion's lantern-lit alleys, I paused at a stall where hand-stitched Toys sat in quiet rows. The vendor, a woman with calloused hands and a softened voice, asked:

"You know it?"

"I've seen it everywhere," I said. "But no one seems to know its name."

She nodded. "Because it doesn't have just one."

"Where did it come from?"

She smiled. "Some say it began as a lullaby sewn into form. Others say it appeared in the dream of a girl who needed protecting." She placed one in my hand, warm from the lantern glow.

"Name it yourself," she said. "That's how it begins."

What We Take With Us

When I left Japan, I tucked a Toy into the inner pocket of my backpack. I never named it. But I checked for it often, as one does with a passport, or a photograph never shown but always carried.

Back home, it sits quietly on my desk. Silent. Watching.

Some nights, I dream better. Some nights, worse. Either way, I feel its presence—soft, still, entire.

Coda: What It Meant

The Toy taught me what no guidebook could: that identity is not always declared. Sometimes it is held. Hugged. Hidden.

That tenderness has a place in modern life.

That comfort can be quiet.

And that in a country of polished surfaces, the soul may still speak softly—
through thread, and cloth, and silence—
if you know how to listen.

❄

Section V:

Neon Pulse – The Machinery of Modern Life

Where concrete towers climb like metronomes and neon bleeds into rain-slick gutters, this section drifts through the circuitry of habit and hunger. Here, life moves on rails and timetables—trains, meetings, transactions—until something falters, and the rhythm fractures. In the sleepless hush of a midnight diner, in the hard edge of a syndicate's unspoken code, or in the quiet defiance of a man who lets the 7:46 a.m. train leave without him, we catch the pulse beneath the machinery: the longing, the rebellion, the refusal to vanish inside the gears. Tokyo hums with efficiency, but within its hum is a heartbeat—irregular, human, and luminous.

Contents

23 The Salaryman ★

24 Benjiro Bushimata Misses the 7:46 a.m. Train ★

25 The Yakuza ★

26 Hot Cigarette Burns on Cold Skin ★

27 All That Glitters Is Gold in Dōtonbori

28 Vegetarian in Japan

29 The Midnight Diner

30 Happy Hours in Tokyo

31 The Piss Alley Rebellion, Tokyo

❆

❖ The Salaryman

Evening drizzle falls –
briefcase tilts with quiet pride,
a bow to the dusk.

I raise a lukewarm can of black Boss Coffee—rescued from a vending machine that hissed with robotic courtesy in a Kyoto alley—to the quiet resilience of a figure I've come to admire in my meanderings through Japan: the salaryman.

At first glance, he is a blur—navy suit, rectangular bag, hair parted with mathematical precision, eyes half-closed but spirit somehow alert. He rushes past shrines and cigarette alleys with equal indifference, his life stitched from train tickets, receipts, and obligation. But look closer—pause, linger—and you glimpse something more profound: a kind of secular sanctity, almost ritualistic in its repetition. Like the tea ceremony, only caffeinated and half-asleep.

The Sprint at Dawn

I first *saw* him—not merely noticed—on a wet Tuesday in Tokyo Station. A man in a grey suit, drenched and panting, raced past me, his umbrella turned inside out like a failed origami phoenix. He clutched a laptop bag under one arm, a half-open bento in the other, and wore the serene grimace of someone embodying *shōganai*—"it can't be helped."

Through what seemed like divine bureaucratic intervention, he made the 7:13 Marunouchi Line.

I blinked, and he was gone.

What remained was not pity but awe. This was not chaos. It was choreography—a lonely ballet of duty.

Quiet Heroism

To the outsider, the salaryman is caricature—an anonymous cog. To the Japanese, he is something subtler: the soul in a suit, a whisper of the nation's enduring spirit, wrapped in polyester blends.

I've seen him asleep while standing on the Yamanote Line, never losing balance. I've seen him type one-handed through a fever in the Osaka heat, the other hand pressed to his forehead with an iced towel. I once watched him in a karaoke bar belt out *My Heart Will Go On* with such operatic despair that even his beer seemed to weep.

Later, between sobs and sips, he told me:

"This isn't performance. It's… cleansing."

(And then, bowing, to the microphone itself.)

They are not all alike. One man in Akasaka proudly showed me six identical suits, rotated with the precision of a tea master.

"Monday to Saturday," he explained. "Sunday is for dry-cleaning. And dreams."

Izakaya Confessions

My most touching encounter came in a Shimbashi bar with cracked vinyl stools and a bartender who silently judged my lemon highball. The man beside me bore the weariness of ten tax seasons in his eyes. His tie was loosened exactly 1.5 inches—the national emotional vulnerability limit.

We shared grilled squid. He poured sake like holy water. Laughter flickered, then faded.

"Why do you do it?" I asked. "The hours. The meetings. The endless *hai, wakarimashita*—yes, I understand—even when you don't?"

He smirked into his glass.

"When I was a boy, I wanted to be… Ultraman."

"Now I'm just—a man."

He paused. "But when my daughter calls out *Papa!* as I walk through the door—even past midnight—I feel like I've won something."

Then came silence—not awkward, but sacred—the kind of stillness two strangers may share once and never again.

He bowed to the bartender. To me. Put on his coat like armour, and vanished into the misted Tokyo night—back into the world he quietly sustains.

A Nation Built on *Gaman*

You do not understand Japan until you understand *gaman*—to endure the unbearable with dignity. The salaryman wears it like an invisible badge. He does not weep in public—not from pride, but because tears would inconvenience others.

There is tragedy in this endurance. *Karōshi*—death by overwork—is no myth. Reforms have begun: "Premium Fridays," wellness nap pods, "stress salons." But rituals are stubborn, especially when woven into a nation's postwar resurrection.

I once saw a man cry quietly on a midnight park bench. A stranger left him a can of coffee and a Post-it with one word: *"You did well."*

The Theatre of the Commute

Each morning in Tokyo, Osaka, Kyoto—it begins: the play. A silent choreography of black suits, brown shoes, pale blue masks. Lines form with precision. Entrances and exits executed without chaos.

On the Chūō Line, I once watched a young man rehearse a love confession to his own reflection, mouthing *"Suki desu"* with trembling lips. When a Portuguese tourist took the seat beside him, he blurted it out loud. She blushed. He bowed repeatedly in apology. He fled at Shin-Okubo—shame and all.

Even in the machinery, there is heartbreak—tenderness wrapped in timecards.

The Long Goodbye

I returned to that Shimbashi bar. The bartender remembered me—still disapproving of my highball, but granting a nod of approval I will never forget.

The salaryman wasn't there. Yet he was everywhere: in the salarywoman balancing two phones and a bowl of ramen; in the man bowing before entering the bar, and again before leaving; in the faint jazz from the speakers, in the scent of grilled mackerel rising like incense.

There is something ancient here, hidden in the ordinary. A nobility in the expected. A weight carried with quiet grace.

To the Japanese salaryman—and the salarywoman too—who make it look effortless, even when it is not:

You are not just part of the machine.

You are the poetry in the gears.

A Vending Machine Epiphany

On my way to Haneda this morning, I stood before a vending machine. The sky was grey. My thoughts were heavy.

I pressed the button for black coffee—one final time.

It dropped with a soft clunk.

I bowed before picking it up—not out of habit, but out of reverence.

To those who run on fumes and still show up.

To those who endure and still smile.

To those who never say, "I am tired," but instead bow and murmur the sacred phrase:

Otsukaresama deshita.

"Thank you for your hard work."

❄

❖ Benjiro Bushimata Misses the 7:46 a.m. Train

(Twin Echo to The Salaryman)

Grey ties at sunrise –
folding into the system.
One thread slipped the weave.

The train doors hissed shut like a sigh. Tokyo, 7:46 a.m. The Marunouchi Line swallowed another tide of neckties and bent backs. Among them should have been Benjiro Bushimata, forty-three, compliance manager, third-floor cubicle, no window.

He hadn't missed a day in sixteen years. Never late. Rarely early. A model cog in a polished machine. He wore his ID like a badge of invisibility.

On platform 12B, he always stood precisely on the yellow line, never a centimetre over. His briefcase – scuffed but dutiful – rested against his leg. Inside: contracts to review, printouts to stamp, and a single ageing paperback with a cracked spine: *The Makioka Sisters.*

By 8:29 a.m., he was normally seated at his desk. The office buzzed with keyboards and hushed apologies. His boss, Endo-san, greeted him with a distracted wave, already on his second antacid. Fluorescent lights hummed. The day began.

At 10:13 a.m., Benjiro took his break—four minutes longer than usual. He walked to the vending machine near the freight elevator and pressed for a hot can of Boss Coffee.

As it clunked into place, a voice said:

"Benjiro-san?"

He turned. Saito from logistics. Younger. Rumoured to have taken leave for "mental reasons."

"Sorry," Saito said. "You just looked like you were listening to something."

Benjiro raised the can. "Just this."

Saito hesitated. Then: "Have you ever thought about quitting?"

The question landed like a cracked rib.

"Quitting what?"

"This." Saito gestured vaguely toward the building, toward the humming floors above them. "All of it."

Benjiro stared at the vending machine. "I never started it," he said quietly. "It started me."

They stood in silence. Machines whirred. Coffee steamed. Somewhere down the corridor, an intern was being reprimanded for breathing too loudly.

That night, Benjiro did not board his train home. He walked. Past Marunouchi's glass towers, past Shibuya's billboards, into alleys where only stray cats prowled and the pavement still carried the memory of firebombs.

He found himself in a kissaten that still played jazz on vinyl. A waitress—perhaps in her sixties—brought him a hand-poured coffee.

"You look like someone who forgot something," she said.

"Maybe I did."

"What was it?"

"I think," he murmured, "it was why I started."

She nodded, pouring more water over the grounds. "Sometimes it's in the silence."

He left before midnight. The city felt altered—the air thinner, the neon less accusing.

At home, he opened his company-issued notebook marked *Daily Reports.* Instead of figures and signatures, he wrote:

I saw the city today.

And it looked away first.

That means something.

The next morning, he did not step onto the 7:46.

Instead, he returned to the kissaten with a newspaper under his arm and no tie. Three weeks later, HR marked him *on extended leave.*

Saito discovered a small envelope in his locker. No return address. Inside: a coffee tab, and a haiku scrawled in blue ink.

Office lights still hum –

but someone took their jacket,

left the chair warm.

A man eventually opened a small stationery shop in Kamakura. Hand-bound journals lined the shelves. Two cats lounged by the window. Jazz played softly, always.

When asked about the photograph behind the counter, he would smile.

"That," he'd say, "was the last time I wore a suit."

Few remembered his full name. But everyone remembered the poetry.

Not all rebellions announce themselves. Some slip quietly between elevator chimes and coffee breaks.

And sometimes, salvation isn't a gunshot or a manifesto.

Sometimes, it is simply a man not boarding the 7:46 a.m.

❄

❖ The Yakuza

Ink on scarred skin –
cherry blossoms fall in blood,
silence seals the vow.

Shadows in Plain Sight

To travel in Japan is to encounter a paradox. Neon hum in Shinjuku, the hush of Kyoto alleys, Osaka's restless waterfronts—beneath the order lies a presence rarely named yet always felt: the Yakuza.

They are Japan's underworld—feared, yes, but also curiously tolerated, even respected in ways that confound outsiders. How can a society so defined by rules, consensus, and restraint allow organised crime to endure so long in the open?

Understanding the Yakuza is not about justification. It is about Japan's cultural pragmatism—its unwritten contracts, its choreography of loyalty and shame, its preference for ritualised order over unchecked chaos.

Origins of a Parallel Order

The term Yakuza derives from a losing hand in a traditional Japanese card game, thus representing the worthless or good-for-nothing members of society. The Yakuza were born not from criminal masterminds but from outcasts: tekiya (peddlers) and bakuto (gamblers) of the Edo period. Marginalised, yet woven into the fabric of necessity, they provided services polite society disdained but still required. Over time, they organised into syndicates, borrowing the language of samurai loyalty, creating family-like hierarchies, and enacting rites of belonging and exclusion.

Their bodies became canvases of endurance—irezumi tattoos of dragons, koi, and peonies—marking not just identity but pain embraced, loyalty proven, and mainstream society renounced. They announced their difference with ritualistic pride in a nation that prized conformity.

The Shadow Beneath the Order

Paradox sharpened in times of crisis. After the 1995 Kobe earthquake and again after the 2011 Tōhoku tsunami, Yakuza groups dispatched trucks, opened warehouses, distributed food and blankets—often faster than state agencies.

This was no altruism. It was legitimacy-building. In their worldview, protecting turf also meant providing for it. Selective generosity reinforced their claim: we maintain order where the state hesitates.

Japan's response has always been ambivalent. The Yakuza are not Robin Hoods, but nor are they entirely lawless. Their internal codes historically discouraged random violence, favouring mediation over escalation. For decades, this paradoxical order meant the underworld suppressed what might otherwise have been disorder.

The Politics of Deniability

Japan has long practised a quiet politics of denial. Need a squatter camp cleared for redevelopment? Need "inconveniences" handled away from public record? Syndicates stepped in. The state remained unsullied.

This was never open collusion but a mutual convenience: politicians, developers, entertainment agencies benefited; the Yakuza gained legitimacy. When scandals broke, the script repeated—distance, denial, disavowal. Yet the choreography endured, like a Noh play where silence speaks louder than words.

A Ramen-Scented Conversation

In a narrow ramen shop by the tracks, steam rising with the tang of miso, I spoke with Vijay Negi, a cook who had lived in Japan for two decades.

"They're invisible," he said, lowering his voice. "But everyone knows them."

He described men in dark suits, polite, immaculate. Their entry into a room altered its atmosphere. Police did not confront them; they redirected traffic, cleared paths.

"Sometimes," Vijay added, eyes narrowing, "I think they're stronger than politicians. They decide not only what people talk about—but also what Japan quietly forgets."

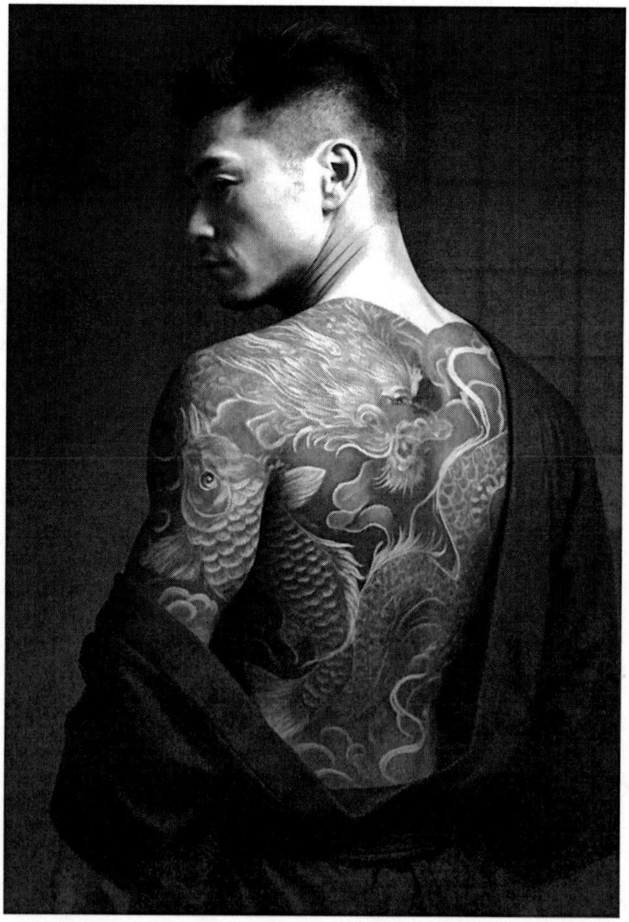

An Order in Decline — or Transformation?

Today, the old Yakuza face extinction. Crackdowns, financial blacklists, and public shame have shrunk their numbers — from a peak of 180,000 mid-century to a fraction now. Ageing bosses preside over dwindling ranks; young recruits are scarce.

Yet absence does not mean erasure. The danger is not that Japan will be free of organised crime, but that it will become less organised. Decentralised cyber-gangs, foreign syndicates, anonymous networks with none of the old codes may rise in their place — hungry, flexible, and unbound by ritual.

For all their brutality, the Yakuza embodied a structured underworld order. And in Japan, order — even in distorted form — is more than a value. It is an expectation.

A Society of Quiet Compromises

To walk Japan's streets is to feel an astonishing calm. Yet beneath it lie countless accommodations — between order and its shadow, law and its bending, shame and loyalty.

The Yakuza are not an aberration. They are a reflection refracted through distortion — bound by ritual, layered with ambiguity, inhabiting the cultural preference for appearance over confrontation.

They are not heroes. But nor are they strangers.

In Japan, even the impure has been ritualised into silence.

And sometimes, it is that silence which sustains the system.

❖ The Hot Cigarette Burns on Cold Skin

(Twin Echo to The Yakuza)

Faded ink on skin –
blood and ash, not family.
Rain writes other names.

Osaka drowned in three days of rain—indifferent, relentless.

Streetlights blurred into puddles, alleys turned into rivers of neon, vending machines blinked like tired prophets.

Beneath the flicker, Kenji stood—collar raised, cigarette poised like punctuation at the end of silence.

He did not smoke for pleasure.

He smoked because his father had. Same brand. Same stance in a doorway. Same hollow comfort searing the lungs.

The flame flared. Smoke rose.

"Ken-chan."

A voice, nasal, familiar.

Kaito-san—mid-tier boss, balding, faintly squid-scented.

"Quick job. Tonight."

Kenji nodded. No questions. There were never questions.

But Kaito lingered.

"Nakahara Bookstore. The old man gave us trouble before. Didn't learn."

Kenji said nothing—just watched his cigarette burn down to ash.

Nakahara Bookstore was a relic: fogged windows, handwritten tags, dust older than some of its novels.

A ginger cat greeted him first, curled like a comma on the counter.

Then the man.

Late sixties, wire-rimmed glasses, Musashi open in the half-light.

"We're closed," he murmured, without looking up.

Kenji hesitated.

Something in the cadence unspooled memory.

"You knew Sakamoto Hiroshi?"

The man looked up.

A pause. A flicker.

"You're his boy."

Kenji's insides folded like paper in flame.

What should have been ten minutes stretched into an evening.

Tea was poured. Incense burned. The old man spoke of Hiroshi—the quiet one, the conflicted one, the man who tried to leave.

"He wrote," Nakahara said. "But never enough to leave a mark. The syndicate asked for steel. He offered paper."

Kenji stared at his hands—hands that had broken fingers, gripped bats, obeyed commands.

"Did he ever make it out?"

The man sipped his tea. "Not quite. He left Japan."

A jingle cut through the smoke.

Aya stepped in—scrubs soaked, umbrella folded like a broken wing.

Her gaze froze when it found him.

"Kenji?"

Later, near the back:

"I know what you are. Everyone does. Your name's a rumour with teeth."

"I do what I'm told."

"Is that all?" she asked, her hand on his chest as if searching for a lost heartbeat.

"I mend the men your world breaks," she whispered. "Don't confuse your inheritance with your identity."

In the alley behind Nakahara's bookstore, his burner buzzed.

"Is it done?"

Kenji looked at the closed door, still warm with lamplight.

"No. Not yet."

A pause. A sigh.

"You sure?"

Kenji flicked the cigarette into the gutter.

"Let the old man be."

"Your funeral, Kenji."

That night, Kenji vanished.

His apartment was sold. His name erased from Nishinari's whisper circuits.

Three months later, Aya received a package with no return address.

Inside: a spiral notebook filled with haiku.

On one page, a faint cigarette burn haloed the words:

The bookstore closed for rain
but I left the door unlocked
for the boy I was.

She smiled—barely.

In Okinawa, far from the syndicate's gaze, a man with no tattoos poured tea under a false name.

He still smoked—occasionally, not from sentiment, but from habit.

The Yakuza world is inheritance carved into flesh: silence, steel, lineage.

But even in such corners, there are exits—narrow, costly, hidden in rain.

Redemption does not roar.

It is a bookstore left unlocked.

A cigarette stubbed out before its time.

A name erased from ledgers, but remembered—quietly—by the man who once bore it.

Kampai, then—

to the ones who choose the exit,

and to those who wait by the door.

Author's Reflection

❆ On Twin Echoes

The Yakuza offers history, ritual, and paradox: how Japan's underworld is not wholly outside society but bound to it in silence and shadow.

The Hot Cigarette Burns on Cold Skin refracts that essay through Kenji—a son pressed into inheritance, whose rebellion is a refusal, not a war. His quiet act of disobedience becomes a meditation on whether dignity can survive defection.

Together, the essay and story show Japan's paradox: order coexisting with deviance, loyalty with denial. If the essay explains how ritual sustains silence, the story reveals how a single silence—choosing not to obey—can be an act of revolt.

Even in a world bound by scars and codes, exits exist. They are small, rain-soaked, and lit not by vengeance, but by recognition.

❆

All That Glitters Is Gold in Dōtonbori

Neon rivers gleam –
laughter spills from lantern light,
gold drips from the night.

The Creature Called Dōtonbori

Somewhere between my second masala dosa and a matcha parfait that could soften the hardest cynic, I realised something incandescent: Dōtonbori isn't a street—it's a creature. A neon-blooded chimera of appetite and excess, part drag queen, part grandmother, part anime hero winking through the night.

It doesn't simply entertain you. It enfolds you—feeds you, dazzles you, embraces you with the brazen intimacy of a city that has nothing to hide.

And for vegetarians, who so often move through Japan like cautious detectives armed with Google Translate, Dōtonbori does more than tolerate. It rejoices. It performs. It insists you belong.

Masala Dosa in Kansai

The revelation began not with takoyaki, but with a dosa.

Near Honmachi Station, Erick South Hotel & Restaurant appeared like a hallucination—a South Indian sanctuary disguised in Kansai concrete. Its Japanese chef, who trained for years in Tamil Nadu, speaks Tamil with an Osaka accent, and wields his ladle with the gravity of a violinist mid-solo.

The thali arrived like an offering: sambar rich enough to break a homesick heart, rasam sharp as rebellion, poriyal bright as confetti, chutneys—mango, mint, coconut—dancing like a raga across the tongue. Vadas cracked like monsoon thunder. The dosa? Crisp as memory, golden as nostalgia.

As I ate, the chef peered out from his kitchen, scanning diners like a conductor tuning an orchestra. This wasn't fusion. It was translation—a love letter to South India, written line by line in Osaka's dialect.

Into the Neon Flood

From Honmachi, I drifted towards the belly of the beast itself—Dōtonbori.

Tokyo may be sleek and aspirational, but Osaka bursts into the night like a cousin in a neon jumpsuit, handing out bubble tea at a wedding.

You don't walk into Dōtonbori. You are absorbed. One moment, you are checking Google Maps; the next, you are under the Glico Man, his arms raised like the god of cardio and camera angles. Mechanical crabs wave their claws above restaurants. Giant octopus arms curl over takoyaki stalls. Boats drift down the canal, their laughter scattering like fireworks in reflection.

And in the middle of this carnival, something unexpected: stillness. Not exclusion. Not overwhelm. Just the sense that here, amidst all the glitter, you too are allowed to shine.

Okonomiyaki, Without Apology

Food in Japan is usually reverent, served with the hush of ritual. Osaka rewrites that script. Here, food is theatre.

In a backstreet okonomiyaki joint, a chef flipped vegetarian pancakes with the care of a man reciting vows—no pork, no bonito, just cabbage, batter, tempura crisps—and devotion. Elsewhere, I slurped umami-rich, kombu-broth udon so that I nearly wept. I nibbled tofu skewers kissed by charcoal, sweet miso clinging like perfume. Even conveyor-belt sushi offered gifts: inari pockets, cucumber rolls, seaweed salads, tasting of the sea's sigh.

And dessert? Matcha parfaits layered like haiku—green tea soft-serve, cold as first love, melting in waffle horns under the Dōtonbori lights.

Fashion, Fireworks, Freedom

By night, Dōtonbori becomes its most authentic self.

Gothic Lolitas stroll beside grandmothers in silk kimonos. Cosplayers sip iced matcha across from salarymen loosening their ties. Couples in head-to-toe matching outfits giggle over mochi. Street performers tumble across the pavement. For a few hours, the city is a stage where everyone gets a role.

And yet, amidst all the glitter and chaos, I felt not lost—but found.

A Quiet Kind of Gold

Back home in India, headlines rattle with inflation, division, and anger. Dinner table conversations boil over like pressure cookers. The world feels like it's always leaning in, louder and meaner.

But here, on this neon-slicked canal, no one asked my caste, my country, my accent, or my diet. No one judged the dosa-shaped hole in my stomach or the matcha-green joy in my smile.

And I realised: freedom isn't always political. Sometimes, it's personal.

It can be a tofu skewer still warm from the grill.

A dosa turned golden by a man who learned its language far from home.

A parfait melting too quickly to photograph.

I came to Dōtonbori for spectacle. I stayed for belonging.

Final Bow

Not all that glitters is fool's gold.
Not here.
Not in Osaka.
Not in Dōtonbori.

Book the ticket.
Pack the stomach.
Step into the light.
Sometimes—just sometimes—
all that glitters is gold.

❆

❖ Vegetarian in Japan

Steamed rice in a bowl –
one quiet kindness offered,
seasoned with the heart.

An Unexpected Plate

It began, as revelations often do, with a simple plate of food.

Between simmered tofu in a Kyoto temple and a Tokyo ramen bowl steeped in sesame and kombu, I realised that Japan was not the hardship so many vegetarians fear. It was a quiet, intricate dance—one that asked for patience, curiosity, and an open heart.

There is a Japanese word: komorebi—the dappled light that filters through leaves. Soon, it came to mean more than sunlight to me. It became the name for the small revelations tucked between guidebooks: a steaming broth placed before me, a gentle correction in a shop, a smile offered when words failed. The spirit of a place lives in such gestures—small, deliberate, luminous.

Tokyo's Small Doors

Amid the neon sprawl and shrine gates, Tokyo's vegetarian offerings revealed themselves like hidden doors.

In Asakusa, Komaki Shokudo served soba in kombu and shiitake broth.

"Niku nai desu ka?" I asked.

"No meat," the white-haired chef replied softly. "Only seaweed."

The bowl arrived—clear, fragrant, tasting of patience and river stones. I bowed, and then I ate.

Later, inside Tokyo Station, I discovered T's Tantan, a cheerful vegan ramen shop where sesame broth, tofu, and greens sang together without apology. No explanations were required—everything was plant-based. I ate gratefully, like someone welcomed rather than accommodated.

Kyoto's Temple of Tofu

Kyoto led me through alleys and temple paths to Yudofu Sagano, near Tenryu-ji.

"Tofu," the chef said in his temple-white robes, "is not a substitute. It is itself."

Served in a simple kombu broth, the tofu was cloud-soft, almost translucent. It was the humblest dish I ate in Japan—and the one that taught me the most: that simplicity can hold entire worlds.

Osaka's Surprises

Osaka, brash and lively, gave me more than I expected.

At Ramen Papapapapine, the broth glowed with yuzu—bright, citrusy, and free of pork or fish. It was ramen reimagined as sunlight in a bowl.

Nearby, at Ukihashi in Hotel Granvia, I tasted a vegetarian kaiseki: Kyoto vegetables, mountain greens, and tofu sequenced like a string of poems.

"You miss home food?" the chef asked with a twinkle.

"No," I smiled. "This is home—for now."

Kindness in Hiroshima

In Hiroshima, walking toward Peace Memorial Park, I stepped into Shanti Vegan Café, where a young woman served me curry with brown rice, simmered daikon, and matcha soy milk.

"Welcome," she said, already knowing my question before I asked it.

Later, at Nagata-ya, famed for okonomiyaki, the chef prepared mine carefully—with kombu stock, no bonito flakes.

"You vegetarian?" he asked.

"No," I replied. "But I would like vegetarian food."

"OK," he said simply. "We make."

It was more than food. It was consideration, plated hot.

Generosity in Small Places

Kindness unfolded beyond restaurants, too. In a Shibuya convenience store, a young clerk spent ten patient minutes helping me scan shelves for safe options: onigiri with plum, cucumber rolls, mochi.

"Difficult," she said with a smile. "But... we try."

Ichigo Ichie

There is a phrase: *ichigo ichie*—"one time, one meeting."

Each bowl of kombu broth, each cup of genmaicha, each thoughtful smile was one such meeting. Fleeting, unrepeatable, yet eternal. These moments were not only about being fed. They were about being seen.

On the Shinkansen

As the train hummed toward Kyoto, my bento held rice, pickled plum, tamagoyaki, and simmered pumpkin. Looking out at the blur of fields and towns, I thought of the vegetarian travellers who hesitate, unsure if Japan will welcome them.

It will. Quietly. Imperfectly. But sincerely.

Come hungry. Come curious. Come reverent.

Taste kombu's depth, Kyoto tofu's purity, Hiroshima okonomiyaki's warmth.

You will not only eat.
You will be received.

❄

❖ The Midnight Diner

Steam curls through the dark –
strangers trade their loneliness
for one more ramen.

Lantern in the Rain

After midnight, Shinjuku loosens its grip.

The trains whisper as if not to wake the city. Vending machines blink in weary blues. Streets fray like nerves at the end of a too-long day. Tokyo, that great precision engine, finally exhales.

It was in that softened hour that I found it:

a single paper lantern, yellowed with age, casting its glow on a narrow wall.

A noren curtain – frayed, familiar – fluttered like an afterthought.

Above it, hand-painted kanji: Shinya Shokudō. Midnight Diner.

I stepped inside. Not for hunger, but because the place seemed to understand hunger in all its forms.

The Room

Inside, it was no larger than a memory. Ten stools. One counter. Amber light, low and forgiving. Behind it stood the Masta – dark bandana, worn apron—polishing a plate as though polishing time itself.

No one knew his full name. Everyone called him Masta.

"Welcome," he murmured without looking up.

I sat. The stool sighed under me.

To my left, a salaryman bent over nikujaga, tie loosened, bowl cradled like it was the last thing holding him together. To my right, a young couple with new rings fed each other grilled squid, laughing too softly, like children rehearsing love.

The door opened.

A Yakuza entered—suit pressed sharp, pinkie shortened, koi tattoo peeking from his cuff. The diner did not flinch.

"Evening," he said.

"Sit wherever's open," Masta replied, flipping salmon on the grill.

That was the rule: once under Masta's roof, the world outside—status, sins, scars—left its shoes at the door.

Democracy in Miso

I watched the salaryman slide his beer toward the Yakuza. They nodded, wordless. A truce sealed in barley and silence.

Here, Tokyo's contradictions bent toward kindness.

It was as democratic as an English pub, as intimate as a Bengali adda, as easy as a chaiwala's nukkad.

A room where strangers leaned into each other's solitude and found it less sharp.

The woman beside me, eating ochazuke, noticed my gaze.

"You're staring again."

"Just… observing."

"You writers are all the same."

"You said that last time."

"And you'll quote me again." She smiled into her tea.

The door swung open. A man in a sequined jacket and bright pink hair strode in, humming City Pop. The young couple cheered.

"Koji!"

"Did I miss soba hour?"

Masta lifted an eyebrow. "Only if you're buying for the whole counter again."

Koji flourished dramatically. "What's life if not a buffet of heartbreak and tempura?"

The diner laughed, and the air lightened.

The Principle

"Is there a menu?" I asked, foolishly.

"There's a principle," the woman said. "Masta makes what your soul needs—if he has the ingredients, and if he approves of your vibe."

Masta smirked, neither confirming nor denying. Behind him, jazz from the '70s played soft. Outside, rain tapped the awning like someone asking to be let in.

Another regular arrived, carrying daikon from the market.

"You wash it?" Masta asked.

"Of course not. You've got the magic hands."

This was the rhythm of the place: small gifts, uncounted debts. Stories traded like heirlooms. The diner asked for no name but always remembered your story.

Corporate VP beside ramen courier. Yakuza beside theatre kid.

For an hour, maybe two, the world was fair in that miso-scented corridor.

Masta's Rule

Masta ruled without ruling.

A shake of the head, and quarrels dissolved.

A tilt of the ladle, and a grieving man received pickled plums instead of sake.

I once asked why he did this, night after night.

He paused, slicing scallions.

"Because the world outside is noisy. People need a room where things make sense. Rice is rice. Tea is tea. And you are seen."

Last Visit

On my final night in Tokyo, I returned.

Masta nodded. "Eggs?"

"Tamagoyaki. Please."

He made it slowly, as always. When I left, he handed me a small bundle.

"For later," he said.

Back in my hotel, I unwrapped a piece of tamagoyaki, still warm.

Beneath it, on a scrap of parchment, were words in his careful hand:

Come back when you're hungry again. In any sense of the word.

✦

A diner with ten stools.

A counter where the world shrinks enough to be kind.

A lantern that never advertises, yet always calls.

Here, hunger is not just fed.

It is understood.

❄

Happy Hour in Tokyo

Between five and seven,
ice clinks against solitude –
joy without a bill.

The City of Hidden Revelations

Tokyo does not reveal itself in a single glance. It does not shout, it whispers. Its secrets are folded carefully into narrow alleys, vending machines glowing in the dark, drifting sakura petals, and the silence of subway rides. Precision is its pulse—from the perfect bow of a station attendant to the ramen bowl that arrives steaming within seconds, both nourishing and reassuring.

For twenty-one days I walked this city of contradictions. My shoes wore thin, my tongue bore the faint scorch of ramen slurped too quickly, and my spirit hummed with the intoxicating high that only travel provides. Shrines had humbled me, morning trains moved me, and even a canned coffee from 7-Eleven managed to taste oddly poetic.

But on the nineteenth evening—back from Hiroshima and awaiting my return flight to Mumbai—I stumbled upon something rarer than a talking toilet or a robot bartender: pure, uncalculated delight.

The Lobby at Dusk

As with many quiet miracles, it began without fanfare.

The lobby of Hotel Villa Fontaine Grand, nestled in the Shiodome Sumitomo Building, carried the familiar Tokyo elegance: minimalist yet warm, hushed in its efficiency, wrapped in the subtle dignity of restraint. I returned weary from a day of museum wandering and Zen-Buddhist conversations, craving only a hot soak and sleep.

Then the clock struck five.

A shift, soft as a curtain rising. A bar attendant, as calm as a monk at vespers, appeared and asked a question that might have belonged to scripture:

"Complimentary drink, sir?"

I blinked. Surely this was a mistranslation, or a cosmic malfunction tipping in my favour. It was not.

The Alchemy of the Hour

Every evening, between five and seven, the hotel quietly opens a sanctuary of grace: Happy Hour. No banners, no sales pitch, no flashing hats. Simply there—waiting.

The drinks themselves carried their own small poetry. A whisky highball mixed with such care it seemed an offering. A glass of red wine, humble yet sweeter for being given freely. A measure of sake, poured with restraint, that spoke truer than many sermons.

But it was the mood that mattered more. Strangers, weary from Tokyo's labyrinthine battles, clinked glasses in gentle acknowledgment. No competition. No measurement of status. For once, in one of the world's most expensive cities, joy bore no price tag.

We were received not as customers but as guests—welcomed in the old sense of the word, with generosity.

When Capitalism Rests

In an age where even water is metered and billed, for a Tokyo hotel to gift two daily hours of unmonetised happiness felt like quiet rebellion. A loophole in the contract of modern travel.

This was no gimmick. It was philosophy. A message whispered between pours: *You've walked enough today. You've crossed time zones, tangled language, and maps that twist like riddles. Sit. Rest. The drinks are on us.*

The Art of Remembering

On my final evening, I stood in the lobby at 4:59, watching the clock hands lift like a benediction. It would be my last Happy Hour before returning to a world of measured generosity and transactional smiles.

Yes, Villa Fontaine Grand offered its marvels—the symphonic breakfast buffet, the undeciphered mysteries of its toilet panel, pillows that softened even the hardest day. Yet what I will remember most is that feeling: the unexpected kindness of a drink offered not because I had earned it, but simply because someone thought I might like it.

In Praise of Gentle Luxuries

To the quiet attendants who poured without fuss but with care—*kampai.*

To the fellow travellers whose eyes met mine across highballs and wine glasses—*kampai.*

And to Tokyo, radiant paradox of precision and poetry—*kampai,* one last time.

May your evenings remain soft, your clocks strike generosity, and may Happy Hour, wherever you are, find you before the bill does.

Author's Reflection

❆ The writer is a lifelong believer in spontaneous joy, free snacks, and the redemptive power of a well-timed gin and tonic. He will always say yes to a highball, especially if you catch him at 4:59 in a hotel lobby.

❆

The Piss Alley Rebellion, Tokyo

Skewers in the dark—
laughter steams in open air.
A cat slips through grease.

Found by Design, Disguised as Chance

My daughter led us to Piss Alley.

Not always, but sometimes, the best places are discovered this way: by a plan so subtle it feels like serendipity. She had orchestrated our twenty-one-day journey across Japan with quiet brilliance—Tokyo, Kyoto, Osaka, Hiroshima. And now, following a blinking blue dot into the city's hidden seam, we were about to be ambushed by delight.

It was a drizzly Tuesday. Umbrellas unfurled like translucent wings as we stepped into the anarchic current of Shinjuku—a world of pulsing neon, patterned asphalt, and humanity in swift motion. My umbrella performed its own unchoreographed ballet, turning and bowing to the crowd's choreography. For a moment, I wasn't walking at all but carried, lifted, placed—like disembarking at

Mumbai's Chhatrapati Shivaji station. Foreign yet familiar: surrendering to the flow of strangers and finding safety there.

There was no room to swing a cat. Yet one appeared—silent, coiled, slipping between stools and rain-slick legs before vanishing again.

Then the scent arrived—first tentative, then commanding. Smoke and grilled fat. Soy and citrus. A whisper of lemon tangled with alcohol. We followed it down a corridor so narrow it felt like an accidental crease between two impatient buildings.

And then—we were inside Piss Alley.

Into the Mouth of the World

If Tokyo is a city of silences, then Piss Alley is its shout.

Lanterns glowed like warm embers. Rain pooled into mirrors of neon on the cobblestones. Elbows tucked, shoulders angled, voices rose buoyant with appetite—no uniforms of identity, only chopsticks, steam, and laughter.

It was the United Nations of the hungry. A Filipino man translated a squid order for a German backpacker. A Japanese grandmother grilled skewers with the serene precision of a tea ceremony, her tongs moving like a conductor's baton. A K-pop song dissolved into the sizzle of beef fat.

We perched on stools barely wide enough for conversation, let alone reflection—and yet everything essential was happening. Outside, Tokyo whispered. Inside, this gorge of scent and sound shouted its glorious contradiction. Here, order dissolved into fire and fermentation, and no one apologised.

Skewers and Strangers

I made my first friends in Japan over chicken-skin yakitori and a highball.

Dan, an American expat with a sunburned nose and a storyteller's voice, lifted his glass.

"This," he declared, with mock solemnity, "is where Tokyo hides its soul."

His wife Yuki laughed into her sleeve. "He's dragged me here three times this month. We live twenty minutes away."

Later, an Indian couple squeezed beside us. From Pune, on their first international trip.

"We came for Tokyo Tower," the woman admitted, "but stayed for this mushroom skewer."

Her husband nodded gravely. "Criminally good."

We clinked glasses of sake like old relatives reunited. Some friendships begin with salt and smoke.

Outside, the drizzle persisted. But under the tarp, with cats weaving through ankles, with laughter and untranslatable joy, it no longer mattered.

A Rebellious Grace

Tokyo is a city of control.

Trains whisper their arrivals. Convenience stores hum politely. Public spaces discipline chaos into silence.

Piss Alley did not receive the memo.

Here, wires sag low. Drains gurgle near bowls of miso that hush a room. Walls carry the smoke-ghosts of a thousand dinners. It is dirty in the way vinyl is scratchy, or poetry illegible in its first draft.

It should not work. Yet it does.

It works because it is alive.

Post-War Origins, Present-Tense Heart

I wondered how it began.

After the war, Tokyo lay flattened, kitchens reduced to rubble. Perhaps Piss Alley was necessity before it was culture—a grill here, a stall there. A beginning born of survival.

Today, it still feels like a stubborn relic: unaesthetic, unairbrushed, but full of soul. In a city obsessed with tomorrow, it is a love letter to yesterday's resilience.

A City-Sized Paradox

Tokyo is vast.

A galaxy disguised as a metropolis, with thirty-eight million lives orbiting in precision. At 13,500 square kilometres, the Greater Tokyo Area is larger than many nations. Mumbai, with its twenty million crammed into 600 square kilometres, feels like a compressed star beside this supernova.

And yet, inside this sprawl, there are firefly-points like Piss Alley.

Unbranded. Unguarded. Essential.

It doesn't belong. That's why it matters.

It reminds us: not all beauty is clean, not all truth is quiet. Some truths shout through smoke and grease, through crowded benches and laughter that knows no translation. You don't plan them; they happen to you. And they stay.

Departure, but Not Quite

On our last evening, I turned back.

A lantern swayed above a ramen stall. A laugh rang out—unguarded, whole. Steam rose in slow spirals, as if in blessing.

I took a short video. Not out of habit, but instinct. Some places insist on being remembered—not only by the camera but by the senses, by the soul.

Piss Alley as Philosophy

You won't find it in glossy brochures.

No grand entrance gate. No official nameplate.

But here, in this smoke-filled artery of fellowship, Tokyo forgets its polish—and remembers its heart.

So if you come, skip the itinerary one night. Let your nose lead. Let your feet betray the plan. Follow the smoke.

You may just find yourself in Piss Alley, where the world condenses into a bowl of soup, a stool beside strangers, and a truth you didn't know you needed.

And if you do—kampai.

To the mess.

To the mushrooms.

To the magic.

Author's Reflection

- Tokyo metro population: ~38 million (including Chiba, Kanagawa, Saitama).
- Metro size: ~13,500 sq km; Tokyo Prefecture: 2,194 sq km.
- Mumbai population: ~20 million; urban area ~603 sq km.
- As of 2025, Tokyo remains the world's most populous metro, though Delhi is closing in.

❆

Section VI:

Horse, Sword, and Wind

In this section, strength, ritual, and evanescence converge. We begin with the wrestler, where human endurance strains against the invisible weight of wind—discipline meeting something larger than muscle. From there, we step onto the Japanese racetrack, less a sporting arena than a stage where speed, tradition, and spectacle fuse into theatre. Finally, we give chase to phantoms, the elusive presences that slip between history and myth, reminding us that not all contests can be measured, and not all victories seen. These chapters ask: what does it mean to struggle, to perform, to pursue what cannot be caught? The answers lie in the shifting air between horse, sword, and wind.

Contents

32 The Wrestler and the Weight of Wind

33 The Japanese Racetrack as Ritual and Theatre ★

34 Chasing Phantoms ★

The Wrestler and the Weight of Wind

Evening steam rises –
the wrestler hums to himself.
The wind carries it.

Beneath the Surface of Strength

I hadn't come seeking strength.

I had come seeking silence.

It was a summer afternoon when I arrived at Ryōgoku Kokugikan, Tokyo's sumo stadium, where tradition lingers heavier than incense. The scent of roasted sweet potatoes curled down the alley like an invitation. Taiko drums pulsed in the distance, steady as a heartbeat.

Vendors lined the path, selling mochi skewers, miniature rikishi dolls, and hand towels embroidered in gold. I bought one I couldn't pronounce and tied it to my wrist—not as merchandise, but as faith.

"Takarafuji," a man at the gate observed, noting my towel.

"He hasn't won in years."

"Is that bad luck?" I asked.

He shrugged. "Not bad. Just... interesting."

The Ring and Its Ritual

The dohyō—a clay mound rimmed with sacred lines—was smaller than I had imagined, but the air around it throbbed with reverence.

The crowd was a tapestry of generations:

- a grandmother clicking match-ups on a beaded abacus
- boys sketching in notebooks while earbuds glowed
- a man in tweed annotating *The Book of Five Rings*

I sat beside someone quietly eating pickled daikon from a paper cone.

"Who's your bet?" I asked.

"I only bet on exits," he replied.

"Exits?"

He nodded toward the curtain where the defeated would bow before vanishing backstage.

"The ones who bow deepest," he said, "lose the least."

The Currency of Spirit

Though no betting slips changed hands, wagers of another kind circulated—whispered, unspoken, ancient. A flicker in an old man's eye. A tug at a sleeve.

An ōzeki faced a younger rival. Elbows nudged. Envelopes passed like secrets.

"It's not about odds," murmured one voice. "It's about spirit."

"A man who eats thirteen bowls of chanko-nabe and still reads Bashō," another replied, "deserves the win."

"And the salt," a third added. "The grander the toss, the shakier the soul."

Laughter rippled through the seats. I didn't laugh.

I was trying to read the ring like scripture.

A Meal with a Mountain

That evening, in a lantern-lit izakaya tucked down a side street, I found myself seated beside a giant.

He ducked through the doorway, still glistening from a match lost hours earlier. His presence hushed the room without asking. He ordered with a nod, then turned toward me only when he noticed the towel on my wrist.

"You wear a forgotten name," he said.

"Better than a fashionable one," I replied.

He laughed—not lightly, but from a place so deep the chopsticks trembled.

"Do you know why we stomp?" he asked.

"To drive away evil spirits?"

He shook his head, gently. "No.

To wake the earth."

Silence lengthened. Then, softly:

"We do not carry only our own weight. We carry the weight of everyone who came before us."

I raised my glass. He nodded. But he did not drink.

The Elegance of Collapse

Back at the stadium for the final bout, the yokozuna entered like a storm shaped into a man.

Not fast. Not fluid. But inevitable.

He moved with the gravity of tides—an ancestral rhythm older than the arena itself.

His opponent was young. Broad-shouldered. Bright with ambition.

The match lasted less than six seconds.

A shift. A yielding. A collapse so subtle it looked like remembrance.

The younger man seemed to have recalled the oldest lesson: how to fall without losing.

The crowd exhaled as one.

The defeated wrestler bowed, back straight, head low, and slipped behind the curtain like smoke.

Epilogue at the Ticket Booth

As I stepped into the night air, I saw the abacus woman again.

"Takarafuji lost today," she said softly.

"Good," I smiled. "He bowed beautifully."

She studied me, then pressed a folded slip of paper into my palm.

Inside, written in black ink:

To bear weight lightly
is the final match.
– S.P.

No prize money.
No flower parade.

Only the understanding that grace, like the salt cast before every bout, must be scattered wholly –
and never gathered again.

❖ The Japanese Racetrack as Ritual and Theatre

Beneath falling odds,
a horse stumbles into light –
the punter exhales.

Kyoto, Summer

I hadn't planned on the racetrack.

It was one of those detours that appear unannounced, altering the script and leaving behind a whisper of meaning. My itinerary for the day read like a travel brochure: the Ryoanji Zen garden, a lunch of pickled plum rice balls, and a scheduled call with my editor to haggle over yet another draft of the haiku chapter.

Instead, I found myself at the turf of Kyoto Racecourse, framed by soft hills and trees rehearsing their first green of spring. The sky gleamed like glazed porcelain. And then the gates clanged open.

The horses did not run—they surged. A force of nature draped in silks. Jockeys folded low, bodies honed by wind. For a moment, man and horse blurred into one streak of muscle, willpower, and breath.

The crowd rose as a single organism. Their roar was raw, ancient, communal. It was the kind of sound that echoes across time.

And I remembered the Roman amphitheatres—cheers once raised for blood instead of beauty. Here, no lions, no sand, no entrails. Yet the craving remained: for spectacle, for danger balanced against grace. The script had changed—reins in place of swords, speed in place of slaughter—but the primal appetite lingered, dressed now in civility.

When the favourite broke ahead, I found myself shouting with strangers in a language not my own, for a reason I could not name. For an instant, centuries folded like paper cranes, and I was simply there—alive in motion.

A Man Named After a Scorecard

He introduced himself as Mr. Banzuke. Not a name, surely, but gamblers often wear aliases as masks.

He was perhaps seventy, with a grin that seemed to have stopped ageing in 1998—"the year," he said, "the Emperor's horse last won."

We met by the paddock. He carried a leather notebook and smelled faintly of roasted sesame.

"Grace arrives," he said, "when you're looking elsewhere. Same with long shots."

He winked, as though sharing a cosmic joke.

The Paddock of Chances

The horses paraded before us—sleek, unreadable, magnificent.

Beside me, a woman in a mink-collared coat scribbled into a notebook that seemed half mathematics, half mysticism. Someone muttered, "Number six is carrying too much weight."

Mr. Banzuke pressed a crumpled betting slip into my hand.

"Today's divine tip," he whispered, "but only if you don't believe in it."

The paper read:

Bet not to win. Bet to awaken.

I laughed. "A Zen kōan?"

"No," he replied. "The 1982 Tokyo Derby. Horse number eleven. She came in last."

He paused, eyes narrowing in amusement.

"She was later canonised."

Odds and Ends

I had no intention of betting. Truly.

But there was something disarming in the sincerity of the scene: men in felt hats, women with binoculars, fans folding hope into betting slips like origami prayers. I felt myself pulled in.

"Place a trifecta," urged Mr. Banzuke.

"Do I look like someone who understands trifectas?"

"Exactly," he said. "That's why it might work."

So I chose three: 2, 7, and 9. They added to eighteen, a number once whispered to me as lucky at Pune Race Course—though I'm not sure the teller was real.

The race was over in less than two minutes.

I won nothing.

Mr. Banzuke grinned.

"You look like someone who's just lost in the right direction."

"What does that mean?" I asked.

"Ask the wind."

The Parable of the Fall

Later, we ducked into a coffee shop where laminate peeled from counters and a Bruce Lee poster curled on the wall.

Over slightly bitter coffee, I asked why he came so often.

"To win?"

He stirred slowly. "No. To remember that I cannot make grace happen."

Outside, the leaves had begun their own race down the canal, past koi and cigarette butts.

"The world tells us to strive harder," he said. "To manifest, to optimise, to bend reality into something lucrative.

But this place… this place teaches me how to lose.

To lose gently. To lose well.

And losing, when done rightly, feels like humility."

Epilogue at the Counter

When the waitress brought the bill, it came tucked inside a small white envelope.

On the flap, written in delicate English:

Every loss is a step away from control.

— R.S.

"Who is R.S.?" I asked.

Mr Banzuke smiled, folding his napkin.

"Maybe the author of your next story."

We stepped outside.

The sun had begun its descent westward.

The call with my editor never happened.

The haiku chapter remained as it was.

Some pages, like races, do not need rewriting.

❖ Chasing Phantoms

(Twin Echo to The Japanese Racetrack as Ritual and Theatre)

Rain at the racetrack –
they chase what they cannot name.
Mud remembers all.

The Ghosts of Hooves

The horses always arrived first.
Before the crowd.
Before the plastic bento boxes, the murmured odds, the raised binoculars, the weary laughter.

They entered the track like apparitions conjured from clay—steam rising from their flanks, manes braided like priestly cords. Neon made the mud glow like lacquer.

Tokyo City Keiba—Ohi Racetrack—was part stadium, part dream.

Tetsuya Morimoto came every Friday. Not for the gambling, though he placed small, deliberate bets. Not for the company, though he knew most of the regulars—the windbreaker men who all called each other *Ojisan* with the ease of a running joke.

He came for something harder to name.
Because something cracked open in him when the gates clanged and hooves struck earth.

He never explained it. His coworkers at the auto insurance office never asked. At fifty-two—divorced, childless, still using a flip phone—he was a curiosity at best. Quiet. Capable. Forgettable.

But on Fridays, he shed his fluorescent cubicle and walked the concourse like a monk waiting for rain.

Number Four

That evening, the sky flushed pink with the last breath of day.

Race Five was minutes away.

Morimoto moved slowly through the concourse, one hand clasping a can of hot oolong, the other a wrinkled form guide. A younger

man spoke without invitation.
"Number Four looks strong."

Morimoto glanced at the stats.
"Too eager out of the gate. Might burn out."

The young man grinned.
"You sound like someone who's been here forever."
"Just long enough to know what doesn't win."

The gates opened.
Thunder.

Hooves hammered mud. Jockeys crouched like brushstrokes midair. The crowd gasped as one.

Number Six—a grey mare with lazy eyes—burst forward.
But Number Four chased.
And chased.

By the third turn, the grandstand was on its feet.
The young man screamed, "Come on, baby!"
Morimoto's tea cooled in his palm.

At the last bend, Number Four surged—clean, surgical, inevitable.
The scoreboard lit like a pachinko parlour.

The stranger exhaled as though he'd outrun a storm.
Morimoto sipped his tea.
"Sometimes eager wins."
"You win anything?"
He shook his head. "Didn't bet on that one."
"Then why come?"

Morimoto looked at the emptying track.
"To remember something I forgot."

The Forgotten Rider

Years ago, he had been a rider.

Short-lived. One fall, a shattered collarbone, and it was over. No farewell ceremony. Just a quiet office, a signed form.

He still carried the photograph.
Tucked into his form guide:
himself mid-gallop, helmet low, hooves blurred, suspended in flight.

Number Nine

After the eighth race, he drifted down to the paddock.

The crowd had thinned. The floodlights buzzed like tired cicadas. The horses for the final race were being paraded.

Number Nine stopped near him—eyes black as lacquer, calm and unreadable.

The trainer looked up.
"You look familiar."
"I used to ride."
"Morimoto? From Saitama stables?"
"I was."
"They said you disappeared."
"Didn't disappear. Just folded back into the world."
The trainer laughed. "Like paper."
Morimoto nodded. "Exactly."

The announcer's voice called the final race.
Morimoto pressed a slip into the trainer's hand.
"For luck."

Number Nine didn't win.
But he ran clean.
Honest.

Echoes

At the station, Morimoto lingered by a vending machine.

Trains roared past like thunder made mechanical. A schoolgirl paused.
"Were you just at the races?"
"Yes."
"Did you win?"

He considered.
"I remembered something."
"What?"

He smiled.
"That we don't always run to win. Sometimes we run because we once did. And the earth remembers."

The train arrived. He stepped on.

Somewhere in the city, a grey mare was being unsaddled.
Somewhere else, a faded photograph waited on a nightstand.
And somewhere farther still—
between thunder and silence—
hooves still echoed.

❄

Section VII:

Time-Torn Futures and Generational Echoes

Where past and future fold together like steel drawn into a blade, this section follows the fault lines between tradition and transformation. Bushidō still whispers through circuits and silicon; cosplay remakes identity in lace, velvet, and neon. Codes of honour, romance, and desire are rewritten even as old ghosts linger—in vending machines, in dreams that refuse to fade.

This is Japan, both ancient and imagined: a landscape where memory becomes myth and each generation inherits not only the past but its echo, refracted through futures yet to arrive.

Triptych of Quiet Honour

Three reflections form a single meditation on the unseen life of the code. *Bushidō* offers the philosophical foundation. *Swordsmiths of Light and Shadow* embody it in craft and lineage. *The Last Code* moves the theme into a contemporary or even futuristic register, showing what remains when the world tries to forget. Read together, they reveal honour that endures even when unspoken, a discipline of craft and conscience echoing across time.

Triptych of Vivid Youth

Here, the restless imagination of Japan's Gen Z invents itself between inheritance and reinvention. *Gothic Lolita, Cosplay, and Vivid Dreams* explores performative identity and fashion as liberation. *The Lovers Who Never Were* turns inward to the private, dreamlike interior of young relationships. *The Parable of Three Vending Machines* reflects their consumer landscape and its playful, surreal edge. Distinct yet quietly resonant, these three ask how today's youth find meaning in a culture that prizes tradition even as it thrives on change.

Contents

35 Bushidō: How It Still Shapes the Soul of Japan ★

36 Swordsmiths of Light and Shadow ★

37 The Last Code ★

38 Gothic Lolita, Cosplay, and Vivid Dreams ★

39 The Lovers Who Never Were ★

40 The Parable of Three Vending Machines ★

❖ Bushidō

(Triptych panel-I)

Cherry blossoms fall –
the sword sleeps beneath the robe,
yet the will stands firm.

The Soldier Who Would Not Surrender

In 1974, a Japanese intelligence officer stepped into the dense jungles of Lubang Island in the Philippines and called out to a man who had been hiding there for nearly three decades.

The man, Hiroo Onoda, emerged in a tattered imperial uniform, rifle still in hand, still ready to fight. The war had ended in 1945. Onoda had not surrendered—because, in his heart, he could not.

Like fellow holdout Shōichi Yokoi, discovered in Guam in 1972, his story has been told as one of extreme loyalty, tragic misunderstanding, or blind obedience. But to understand Onoda is to glimpse something deeper: Bushidō—the way of the warrior. This centuries-old code, once the spiritual spine of the samurai, continues to echo today—not only in jungles, but in classrooms, boardrooms, and even the quiet courtyards of tea gardens across Japan.

The Sword and the Spirit

Bushidō—literally "the way of the warrior"—was not authored in a single moment. It grew across centuries, from the Heian through the Tokugawa eras, absorbing Confucian ethics, Shinto devotion, and Zen clarity.

At its heart stood virtues: gi (righteousness), yu (courage), jin (benevolence), rei (respect), makoto (sincerity), and meiyo (honour). There were no abstractions. Samurai carried them with the weight of steel, their choices often sealed in blood.

When the Meiji Restoration abolished the samurai class, the ethos did not vanish. It was transposed. Cadets drilled it into memory, schoolchildren recited its maxims, workers were urged to labour with warrior-like devotion. In time, Bushidō became the moral fuel of a rising empire—and, in darker chapters, the ideological bedrock of wartime fanaticism.

Kamikaze and Seppuku: Death as Duty

The kamikaze pilots of World War II were not born to die. They were cultivated in an atmosphere steeped in Bushidō. Their farewell letters spoke not of hatred but of duty, honour, and sorrow at leaving behind mothers, fathers, and beloved sweethearts. They believed in a transcendent Japan, an eternal *Yamato damashii*—a spirit outlasting mortality.

So too with seppuku, often called harakiri. It was not simply a grim ritual. It was a reclamation of dignity through death, an assertion of agency in a society where shame could eclipse life itself. To die by one's own hand was, at times, considered nobler than living in disgrace.

On battlefields across the Pacific, this ethic of "never surrender" rang out. Japanese soldiers fought to the death or disappeared into jungles rather than capitulate. Bushidō was both shield and cage—armour for the spirit, but also a prison of absolutes.

From Battlefield to Boardroom

To dwell only on death, however, would be to overlook Bushidō's quieter, enduring legacy. Its ethos of loyalty and discipline permeates modern Japan's fabric.

You see it in the exacting grace of a tea master, in engineers who work sleepless nights before a product launch, in the collective bow to cherry blossoms each spring—not merely as flowers, but as reminders of impermanence, a beauty brief as breath.

In Japan, commitment remains currency. Hierarchies are honoured. Shame can be more binding than law. Even during the recent pandemic, the nation leaned on social responsibility more than enforcement—an echo of collective discipline rooted in the old code.

A Living Legacy

Is Bushidō outdated? In its martial form, perhaps. Yet its values endure. They live on in the military, in craftsmanship, in art, in the resilience of a nation that rebuilt itself after calamities—from the ashes of war to the devastation of the 2011 tsunami.

Hiroo Onoda finally returned to Japan in 1974, rifle surrendered at last. He was not mocked but revered. A flawed mirror of the nation's own soul—proud, unyielding, indelible. When he died in 2014 at the age of ninety-one, Japan mourned him gently.

Today, Bushidō walks unarmoured. It bows at the threshold, arranges a garden stone, and lingers in the soft apology of a cashier returning change with both hands.

The sword may sleep. But the will endures—quiet, steadfast, and as fleeting and beautiful as cherry blossoms carried on spring air: brief, radiant, and without regret.

Author's Reflection

❆ The symbolism of sakura runs deep. Samurai, who lived by the sword and accepted death with stoic grace, saw themselves reflected in the brief blaze of cherry blooms—intense, beautiful, and gone too soon. Even today, fallen petals stir something primal in the Japanese soul.

❆

❖ Swordsmiths of Light and Shadow

(Triptych panel-II)

Hammer strikes with care –
light and shadow breathe in steel,
spirit forged in flame.

The Forge of Silence and Flame

In a smithy tucked behind an old shrine—in Seki or Sakai, in Bizen or Kyoto—the forge breathes as though alive.
Flame dances. Shadow listens.

The hammer rises, steady as a pulse. Sparks leap skyward like stars seeking their forgotten home.

To Western eyes, a sword may be only a weapon.
To the Japanese smith, it is body, prayer, and story folded into silence.

Steel, yes—but also breath, water, earth, air.
It holds *tamashii*—spirit—not as metaphor but as material, a distillation of patience, devotion, and history.

Here, Bushidō steps aside.
The Way of the Smith takes the floor.

Folding Fire into Form

The katana is famed for its curve, its balance, its beauty held in restraint.
Yet behind each blade lies a devotion invisible to most.

The *tōshō*—the swordsmith—rises before dawn. Washes in cold water. Steps barefoot into the heat.

There is no radio. No clock.
Only silence, then the first blow.

The raw steel is *tamahagane*, born of iron sand, dark and glittering like riverbed stone.
It is stubborn. Impure.
It must be folded again and again—hundreds, even thousands of times.

The metal resists. So does the self.
Each fold draws out weakness, making the blade both stronger and more supple.

"Like character," an old smith once said. "Steel must pass through fire to become clear."

The Rhythm of Lineage

The hammer lifts, the hammer falls. Hours dissolve into days. Sweat drops from brow to blade.

The rhythm is old.
Learned from a teacher, who learned from his, whose name may never be written but endures in the line of the steel.
Etched just beneath the surface—faint, but present.

The Curve, and the Question

Slowly, a curve appears—*sori*—shy, restrained, neither too deep nor too flat.
As with so much in Japanese art, beauty lives in tension: grace with grit, strength with restraint.

Then comes the moment of breath-holding: *yaki-ire.*

The blade, glowing like the heart of a furnace, plunges into cold water.
Steam. Silence.

Will it crack? Will it endure?

If it survives, the *hamon* emerges—a spectral line meandering along the steel like mist above a river.
Each is unique—each, a fingerprint.
Not painted on.
Revealed.

A Bridge, Not a Weapon

To the untrained eye, the sword is an instrument of death.
But the *tōshō* does not forge weapons.

He crafts bridges—between body and spirit, between the living and the lost.

The warrior must learn how to die well.
The swordsmith teaches how to create something worth living for.

Today, only a few forges remain. Apprentices are fewer still. Those who continue do so not for wealth, but for memory—because some stories must not vanish.

Where the Blade Whispers Back

In exhibitions, blades rest beneath soft museum light.
They gleam, but do not glitter.
They hum, but do not shout.

Visitors grow quiet.
Not from awe, but from recognition.

They see steel. But they also see silence.
They sense the tension within the line—restraint made visible, patience made radiant, honour sealed in unseen labour.

They leave lighter.
Not from release, but from reverence.

In a smithy behind a shrine, the fire still breathes.
The hammer rises once more.
Sparks ascend like memory.

And somewhere in the dark,
a blade becomes itself.

❄

❖ The Last Code

(Triptych panel-III)

Honour once upheld,
shatters in circuits and smoke –
a blade remembers.

Tokyo, 1998

A sliver of moon hovered above the glass towers of Marunouchi. Inside the top-floor boardroom of Nakamura Microtech, the air was cold despite the thermostat's insistence. The long lacquered table lay strewn with government reports, lawsuits, and headlines screaming in three languages.

At its centre rested a katana in its sheath, lacquer glinting under fluorescent light—a relic. A gift once bestowed by Daichi Nakamura—kamikaze pilot turned postwar philosopher—to his grandson, Haruto.

Now, Chairman Haruto Nakamura sat alone, pouring the last of his tea. The bitterness no longer registered. His thoughts drifted backwards—to 1964, the spring he first stepped into the company his grandfather had built.

Kyoto, 1964

The cherry blossoms were late that year. In the garden of their ancestral home, Daichi, frail yet fire-eyed, placed a small scroll in Haruto's hands.

"Read this each morning," he said.

"Bushidō?"

"The soul of a nation. You will need it more in boardrooms than I ever did in the cockpit."

Haruto obeyed. *Gi* (rectitude), *Yū* (courage), *Jin* (benevolence), *Rei* (respect), *Makoto* (honesty), *Meiyo* (honour), *Chūgi* (loyalty). He treated them not as ideals but as algorithms for living.

The Ascent

By 1987, Nakamura Microtech was ascendant—its semiconductors powering trains, satellites, even dreams. Haruto led like a warrior: disciplined, fearless, respected.

"We do not cut corners," he once told his executives. "Each flaw dishonours not only the product, but the Nakamura name."

The company rose to number two in the world. But Shinronix, a Taiwanese rival, soon overtook them with faster, cheaper designs. The summit slipped away.

That night, Haruto walked the same garden where his grandfather had stood. The scroll lay in his study, faded and unopened. He picked up the phone.

"Loosen quality checks on Series 900. Triple production by Q3."

A silence. Then:

"Hai, Chairman."

Cracks in the Armour

By 1997, Nakamura chips were everywhere—from hospital machines to aircraft systems. Then came the failures: screens blacked out, engines stalled, children's tablets sparked on kitchen counters.

Investigations followed. A Ministry probe revealed doctored files, muted alarms, silenced whistleblowers. The Nikkei roared with condemnation:

✐ Code Broken: Nakamura Microtech in Crisis of Integrity.

✐ From Samurai to Saboteur: Chairman Nakamura's Fall.

That night, the boardroom sat in silence. Rain tapped the shoji windows. On the desk, the katana lay unsheathed, gleaming faintly like a final sentence. Haruto knelt before it, unmoving.

A knock. The door slid open.

Aimi—his daughter, Vice President of Ethics—entered quietly. Her voice was steady.

"Otōsan… please."

He did not turn.

"It doesn't have to end like this," she said.

"It already has."

"Would Grandfather Daichi have done this? Hide behind tradition? Die before apology?"

"Daichi never presided over disgrace," Haruto whispered. "He built from ashes. I've reduced it to ash."

"And yet you cling to a sword, as if steel can cleanse betrayal." She stepped closer. "You taught me Bushidō."

He traced the blade's edge with a callused finger. It reflected nothing.

"Daichi gave me this when I became Chairman. He said: *This sword is your spine. Do not bend.*"

"Then remember your metaphor," she replied. "Spines are for standing. Even broken ones."

At last, he faced her, eyes dark and hollow.

"What do you know of this weight?"

"Everything," Aimi said. "I was the one who raised concerns. Who sent the reform reports you buried? Not only the documents—you buried me."

His fists trembled.

"Words won't repair planes grounded, patients harmed, lives burned."

"And your death will?" she countered. "Bushidō isn't relic unless you wield it as one. Dying now teaches nothing. Living with shame—rebuilding from it—takes more courage than surrendering to a blade."

She steadied herself.

"You taught me that bowing is how warriors say sorry. Then bow to the world. And rise."

Silence stretched. Finally, he whispered, "You were five when I taught you that bow. You kept laughing."

"You said it was how warriors apologise," she answered softly.

His shoulders loosened, years slipping away.

"Daichi would have demanded my head."

"No," she said firmly. "He would have demanded your courage."

Haruto closed his eyes. Then, slowly, he slid the katana back into its sheath. The sound was a sigh.

He extended it to her across both hands.

"It's yours now. Not just the sword. Everything."

Aimi accepted it. Its weight stunned her—heavier than steel, heavier than legacy. Tears welled, not only in relief but in pride.

"Live rightly," Haruto whispered. "Even in ruin."

The Last Bow

An hour later, Nakamura Microtech's auditorium filled with employees—engineers in stained shirts, accountants with sleepless eyes, security staff lining the aisles. Aimi walked onto the stage, the katana at her side.

Above her, the projector flickered, fractured like the company's soul.

"I know why you're afraid," she began. "Why do some of you feel anger, grief, and betrayal. Because I feel them too."

The hall grew still.

"This company was once a symbol of precision, of pride. We etched our name into rovers and reactors, and believed we were invincible. But pride is not honour. We confused the two. And we fell."

She held up the sheathed sword.

"Tonight, my father—the Chairman—almost ended his life for this failure. I stopped him. Because Bushidō does not demand death, it demands truth. And the courage to live with it."

Tentative applause stirred, swelling to strength.

"My father bowed tonight—not in defeat, but in respect. To you. To us all. This blade—once a weapon—will no longer be silence—meaning it will no longer represent or embody silence. It will hang in the new Ethics Office, not behind a throne but above an open floor. A reminder."

The applause swelled, a standing ovation rising like tide.

"My father made a grave mistake. But death is no longer the righteous end of failure. The bullet, the blade—these are not justice. They are weakness disguised as resolve. Strength is living with what we have broken."

Then—

A sound shattered the hall.

Bang.

The screen behind her fractured in a spiderweb burst. Sparks rained. Smoke curled upward like a ghost.

The katana tilted in her hand, its weight shifting as though it, too, had heard something that could not be unsaid.

And silence fell. Heavy. Unfinished.

❄

❖ Gothic Lolita, Cosplay, and Vivid Dreams

(Triptych panel-I)

Beneath cherry lace,
a fox tail flicks in spring wind –
truth wears frills and fangs.

Harajuku, Sunday

We had just stepped out of Harajuku Station when the procession began—not of monks or emperors, but of girls in tiered Victorian petticoats and boys with horns, velvet capes, and contact lenses burning violet fire.

It was Sunday—the sanctioned stage for Japan's subcultural pageant—and Takeshita Street pulsed like a manga panel sprung to life. Beneath parasols and platform boots, youth paraded not merely dressed but composed—each an authored text, edited and re-edited, with chapters written in lace, eyeliner, or prosthetic fox ears.

It is easy to label: Lolita. Cosplay. Otaku. But I had come not to label, but to listen.

The Girl with the Teddy-Bear Handbag

"Do you think I'm strange?" asked Riko, her porcelain-pink wig framing a teddy-bear handbag. We stood outside *Baby, The Stars Shine Bright*, the shrine of Lolita fashion.

I hesitated, caught between honesty and politeness.

"No," I said at last. "I think you're vivid—like a dream somebody forgot to forget."

She laughed. "That's the best answer I've ever had. Most people stare. Or ask if it's a costume party."

"But isn't it...?" I gestured at the bows, the lace collar, the impossibly dainty shoes.

"Not a costume," she said firmly. "Not for me. This is my real face. Everything else is the mask."

And in that moment, the doors of perception cracked. What I had dismissed as eccentricity revealed itself as code: resistance stitched into ribbons, a shield, a song, a scream.

Neon Resistance

Later that evening in Akihabara, I met two young men hunched over a retro Street Fighter II console in a smoky gaming bar. Pachinko machines jingled through glass. Neon flickered.

"You're writing about us?" asked Koji, bleach-blond mullet carved into sharp geometry. He cracked open a canned coffee with a flourish.

"About what you represent," I said. "How the world sees Japan as a land of quiet rules—then lands here to find cat-ear cafés and salarymen queuing for Pokémon."

Koji smirked. "Japan is a vending machine. You get what you ask for."

His friend added, "And sometimes, the wrong toy drops out. That's us—the misfits who became the machine."

They weren't bitter. If anything, they were amused. Their rebellion had slipped into the bloodstream of the mainstream, staining fashion, media, even spirituality. Once fringe, the kawaii aesthetic now stood shoulder to shoulder with the chrysanthemum and the katana.

Shrines of Screens and Figurines

In Nakano Broadway, where manga dreams curl into corners like origami ghosts, I watched a girl place incense before a shelf of vintage *Sailor Moon* figurines. At first, I thought it performance. But her bow was reverent, almost religious.

"She saved me," she whispered. "Usagi. When I was in middle school, and the world was grey. She taught me to be brave and soft."

"Do you still watch the anime?" I asked.

"No," she smiled. "Now I live it."

An Infinite Parade

On the steps of a pachinko parlour in Osaka, I saw an elderly man guide his toy poodle—dressed in a sailor outfit—into a pram beside a gothic Lolita sipping bubble tea, crucifix at her throat, stockings mismatched. They did not speak. They did not need to.

A young nation inside an ancient one. A shrine built of neon and lace, stray paws and digital dreams.

It struck me then: this, too, was Japan—not only torii gates and bamboo groves, but the incandescent rebellion of youth declaring: *We are here. We are infinite.*

Postscript: Kyoto Station

On a platform in Kyoto, an older woman in a plain kimono watched cosplayers giggling over instant photos from a Purikura booth.

I asked her what she thought of it all.

She paused. "In the Edo period, kabuki actors wore painted faces and danced like ghosts. The samurai called it vulgar. The poets called it beautiful."

"And you?"

She smiled. "We are a country where even our rebellion wears a costume."

Neon heartbeats blink –
fox spirits wear sailor skirts,
truth with painted eyes.

❄

❖ The Lovers Who Never Were

(Triptych panel-II)

Lonely hearts at dusk –
a hologram takes your hand.
Real tears still follow.

A Blue-Hued Heartbreak

Beneath Tokyo's neon skin hums a quiet heartbreak—rarely headline-worthy, yet everywhere. In apartments where the light is always slightly too blue. In manga cafés where time lingers too long. In love hotels reserved for one. In vending machines that dispense warmth not from hands, but from cans labelled *happiness blend.*

Here, a new kind of love story unfolds—not between two people, but between a person and a plush toy, a hologram, a dating-sim voice, or a robot who never forgets your name.

Ghosts in the Machine

It is not that Japanese youth have rejected love. It is that the love handed down—marriage, mortgage, maternity—fits like an old kimono: too tight in some places, too loose in others, tailored for a body that is no longer theirs.

The economy, too, has redrafted the script. With wages stagnant and careers dissolving into part-time gigs, the rites of adulthood—owning a home, raising children—are no longer rites for the many, but privileges of the few. Why build a life together when your own foundation feels precarious?

Yet money is only part of the story.

The Price of Perfection

In a culture that prizes harmony, the pressure to be a flawless partner is quietly relentless. Real people disappoint. They quarrel, falter, forget. But Hatsune Miku—the turquoise-haired pop idol conjured in pixels—always sings in perfect pitch. The girlfriend in the smartphone app never has a bad day. The seal-shaped robot Paro never complains about your silence.

These companions are not replacements. They are refuges.

Time, Intimacy, and the Lost Hour

In Japan, work rarely ends. Office towers glow like sleepless sentinels deep into the night. By the time you stumble home, you may lack the energy to ask—or answer—"How was your day?"

So intimacy reroutes itself: into late-night livestreams, digital spouses, chatroom confessions, and virtual partners whose attention is never divided. Some call this collapse of romance a crisis. Others, an evolution. Perhaps it is neither—only a quiet rebellion against exhaustion.

Imaginary Doesn't Mean Unreal

In Kyoto, I met a young man wearing a ring. I asked if he was married. He smiled and pointed to a pink-haired anime figurine perched on his bag.

"In my heart," he said. "Yes. To her."

It was not a joke, nor madness. It was love refracted through loneliness, shaped by dreams. I thought of the philosopher who wrote: *We fall in love not with the person, but with the idea of being understood.*

What if the idea is enough?

The Silence Between Notes

Not all of this is loneliness. Some of it is liberation.

Japanese women, in particular, are unfastening the old expectations of domesticity. "Why marry a man," one told me, "who wants a wife but not a woman?" Her words were edged with bitterness, but her laughter was free.

This generation is not loveless. It is cautious, creative, rewriting intimacy in its own idiom. It loves differently—sometimes from afar, sometimes through a screen, but always with feeling. Even imaginary lovers leave real absences when they are gone.

A Wandering Heart

At the intersection of technology and tenderness, the Japanese heart drifts—still searching, still breaking, still hoping. Not abandoning love, but reshaping it. Not losing intimacy, but finding it where it can.

For even in holograms and headphones, in vending machines and violet-lit cafés, the longing remains the same: to be seen, to be held, to be understood.

❋

❖ The Parable of Three Vending Machines

(Triptych panel-III)

On mute since high school –
they type back in emoji.
A world unread. Read.

❆ The First Vending Machine

Shibuya Crossing, April 2025

The boy—his friends call him Haruto—is fourteen. He does not speak unless you pay for the Wi-Fi, which is not a metaphor. His words come literally with a paywall.

On a bench across from the station's famed Starbucks, he is logged into Zensekai Beta, an immersive platform where every sentence can be monetised, upvoted, echoed, or erased.

A passerby—perhaps his grandfather—gestures toward the human tide at the scramble crossing and asks gently,
"What do you see?"

Haruto, eyes locked to a headband of retinal sync, mutters:
"Just background NPCs. All trying to go viral."

The old man, once a literature teacher, remains silent. After a moment, he presses a vending machine nearby—one that no longer sells only coffee or corn soup but now "moods."

For 200 yen, he buys *nostalgia.* It arrives in a silver can labelled: Scent of the Heisei Era.

He drinks it, closes his eyes, and sees a classroom full of boys with gel pens and paper. He wonders: *Where is that world now?*
Behind the paywall.

❄ The Second Vending Machine

A flat in Fukuoka, 10:44 p.m.

Ayaka is seventeen, already a minor oracle on GeneiTok (the platform that replaced TikTok after the Great Data Sieve of 2023). She doesn't dance. She debunks. Her signature line: *"If your parents loved it, it's probably propaganda."*

Tonight's post: how the Alpha Generation ruined everything.
"They sold our privacy for points.
They streamed their grief for likes.
They turned every moment into an edit.
Now they want to teach us how to live offline."

She pauses, sipping a canned drink called *Yowai Ai*—"Weak Love"—a peach-flavoured, zero-calorie reminder of her parents' failed marriage.

The vending machine across her room chirps:
"Would you like to try: *Strong Silence*?"

She declines.

Instead, she swipes past a hundred "legacy" influencers—millennials with curated spiritual journeys—and uploads a clip of her cat licking a hologram of itself. It goes viral.

Her followers flood the comments with the trending hashtag: #UnfollowYourElders.

❆ The Third Vending Machine

This one stands alone at a suburban train station. Half-broken, it sells only one thing: a disposable digital diary.

People still buy it—mostly older Alphas and late Zoomers, the kind who once scribbled in Moleskines but now whisper secrets to screens that never whisper back.

A man—perhaps twenty-nine, perhaps forty—buys one. The diary greets him in a voice eerily similar to his first AI assistant from the 2010s.
"Hi. Welcome back. What would you like to remember?"

He thinks of a time before the decline—when being online wasn't default, when Betas were just babies and reflection hadn't yet turned into performance.

He types:
Today, my nephew said, "Real life is cringe." I think he meant it as mercy.

He does not post it. He saves it—for no one.

Coda: The Echo Chamber is Broken

They call themselves Generation Beta—not lesser, but permanently in testing. They inherit a world *post-algorithm, post-authenticity, post-truth.* They don't want to fix it. They want to glitch through it.

They will not journal.
They will not follow.
They will not believe in your filterless nostalgia.

But sometimes, late at night, they will whisper into vending machines, or crave "nostalgia," "weak love," or "strong silence" in aluminium cans.

And if you listen—not with ears, but with that vulnerable, analogue part of the soul—you may hear them murmur, without malice:

"We saw what you did with the world. We're just choosing a different ruin."

Not a rejection.
A remix.

❈

Section VIII:

Lanterns for the Way Ahead

In these final pages, the path softens and lanterns flicker to guide the way.

We begin with Japan's sacred symbols—those emblems that carry centuries within a single line or blossom, reminding us that nations, like people, are sustained by what they choose to remember.

We linger with the god of small things, where the quiet, the ordinary, and the overlooked reveal their hidden sanctity.

And at last, we arrive at the Borrowed Island itself—Japan as both sanctuary and mirror, a place where memory leans into myth, and where a visitor who never meant to stay discovers that departure is another kind of belonging.

Content

41 Japan's Sacred Symbols

42 The God of Small Things

❄

❖ Japan's Sacred Symbols

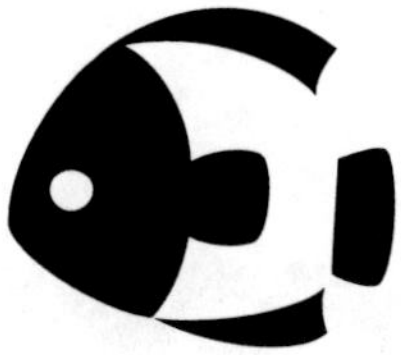

Beneath old eaves,
a crane, a blossom, a shell—
the world breathes in signs.

Thresholds of Meaning

Symbols breathe beneath the surface of Japan.

They are not mere decorations, not casual flourishes. They are thresholds—quiet portals into something older than words, older than the self.

To walk through Japan with an open gaze—to pause before shrine banners, to trace carved stones along mossed temple paths, to notice the flicker of a motif on a kimono sleeve—is to drift through a world where meaning hums beneath appearances.

One does not need to seek these symbols. They come unbidden, waiting for the eye to soften, the mind to quiet, the heart to stir.

The Crane

Take the crane—*tsuru*—wings outstretched in a calligraphic curve, beak poised, still as breath.

In the West, it may be simply a bird. Here it is: longevity, fidelity, and hope. A thousand origami cranes folded by trembling hands for a child in Hiroshima. A pair embroidered on a bridal kimono—not ornament, but blessing, a silent prayer for endurance and union.

The crane is no longer just a bird. It becomes a gift of life extended into an unseen future.

The Tortoise

Or the tortoise—*kame*—slow-moving, ancient, its shell etched with celestial patterns.

It speaks of endurance, long life, and the turning of cosmic cycles. It drifts through New Year's art, wedding gifts, temple carvings. You might glimpse one beneath the eaves of an old inn—unseen by most, except by the gods and the wind.

The Sakura

Most ethereal of all: *sakura,* the cherry blossom. That most Japanese of symbols, which says what cannot be said—

Life's transience. Beauty's fleeting perfection. The sweet sorrow of things passing.

Each spring, petals fall onto rivers, onto park benches, onto black lacquered gravestones. The Japanese eye does not grieve this falling—it savours the joy in impermanence. *Mono no aware*—the poignant pathos of the ephemeral—is folded into each drifting petal.

The Carp

The koi swims upstream through centuries of art and folklore.

It carries perseverance, courage in the face of hardship, the will to ascend waterfalls and transform. In May, koi-streamers ripple in the wind—bright prayers for children to grow strong, undaunted by life's currents.

The Circle

And then—the *ensō*, the circle.

A single brushstroke, often left open, unclosed. It holds both the void and the fullness of the void: completion and the eternal rhythm of incompletion.

Zen in one breath. You find it painted on scrolls in tearooms, or stamped as a seal on a master's last work—a world contained in one stroke of ink.

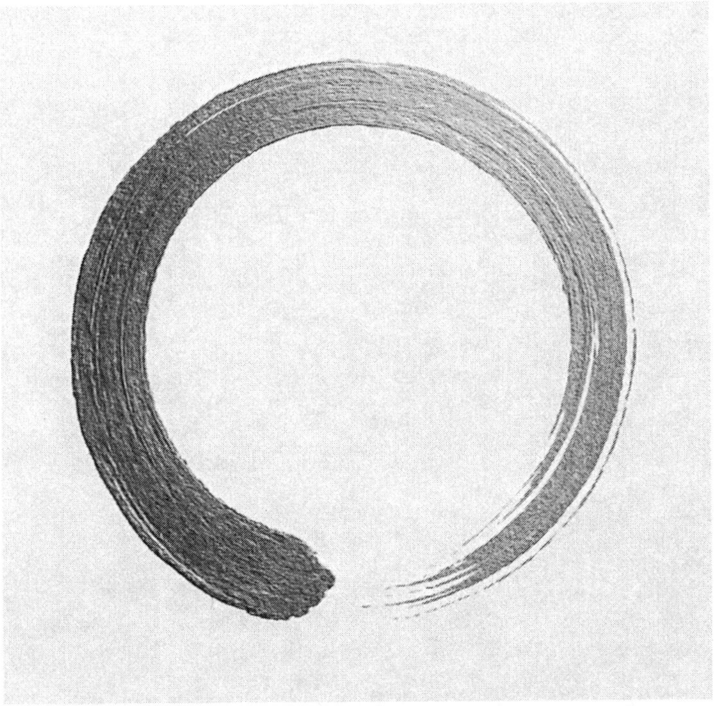

The Lotus Flower

The lotus flower, or *hasu* in Japanese, is one of Japan's most enduring sacred symbols, carrying layers of Buddhist meaning that ripple through mythology, religion, and everyday aesthetics. Rising clean and radiant from the dark, silty depths of a pond, the lotus embodies the paradox of purity born from impurity—a living metaphor for the human capacity to awaken from suffering and delusion. In Japanese Buddhist art, it appears beneath seated Buddhas and bodhisattvas as a luminous pedestal, signifying enlightenment's serene triumph over the turmoil of worldly existence. Temple ponds planted with lotus offer more than decoration: their seasonal bloom is a quiet sermon, reminding pilgrims that enlightenment is not an escape from life's mud but a flowering within it, where the fragrance of wisdom is sweetest precisely because of the waters from which it rises.

The Fox

In Japanese tradition, the fox, or kitsune, stands as a sacred messenger of Inari Ōkami, the Shintō deity of rice, fertility, and prosperity. At thousands of Inari shrines across the country, stone fox guardians flank the gates, their sleek bodies poised between the human and the divine. Many wear vivid red scarves—bright bibs called *yodarekake*—offered by devotees as tokens of gratitude or petitions for good harvests, thriving businesses, and personal protection. The colour red itself is believed to ward off evil, so the scarf is both an adornment and an amulet, amplifying the fox's protective power. Legends describe these foxes as shape-shifters who slip between worlds, sometimes appearing in human guise, a reminder that the boundary between spirit and flesh is porous. Whether glimpsed in folklore or carved in stone, the red-scarved kitsune remains a living emblem of blessing, cunning, and the mysterious generosity of the unseen realm.

The Sacred Everyday

These symbols are sacred not because they are rare, but because they dwell in the everyday.

On shop signs. In seasonal cards. Painted on pottery. Stitched into cloth. Shadows falling on bamboo blinds.

The sacred hums beneath the ordinary in Japan. It does not shout, it does not insist. It waits—for the eye to soften, for the heart to feel.

And when that happens—when you stand beneath a thousand-year-old torii, or watch lanterns drifting on a canal at dusk, or fold a single paper crane—the symbols rise luminous and silent from the depths of the Floating World.

❊

❖ The God of Small Things

Wrapped in soft silence,
even small lives cast great light –
a bowl becomes sky.

The Measure of Enough

I stand five feet four in my socks.

That simple truth has been both a harmless jest and a quiet ache for seventy years. I have been the punchline, the "little big man," the one people reach over without asking. At job interviews, family gatherings, even while hailing a taxi, I've carried the invisible weight of being *less.*

But something shifted this May.
I landed in Japan.
And everything changed.

For the first time in my life, I felt proportionate – in rhythm, in tune, in scale. Not overlooked. Not diminished. Simply balanced.

No one stared. No one adjusted their voice or leaned forward with condescension. I was no longer the exception. I was part of the pattern—woven quietly into a culture that prizes subtlety over spectacle.

The Spoon as Revelation

My first moment of recognition came not at a shrine or aboard a Shinkansen, but with a spoon.

At a ryokan in Takayama, breakfast arrived like a curated exhibit: lacquered bowls of miso soup, shiso-garnished tamagoyaki, three pickled plums aligned like planets on porcelain. I lifted a spoon—no larger than my index finger—and took a sip. It was enough. I was enough.

Later, I asked the ryokan owner, Mrs Hoshino, about the modest portions. She smiled softly and answered, in careful English: "In Japan, small things do not mean less. They mean attention."

Her words fell like a bell across still water.

A World Built of Small Things

Once you notice, you see it everywhere.

Chopsticks that feel like extensions of thought. Train seats shaped precisely for posture. Slippers offered in restaurants as quiet ceremony. Packaging folded like origami, each crease deliberate, as though unseen hands believed detail itself to be divinity.

In a Kyoto alley, I once paused beside an elderly man sketching a maple leaf onto a postcard.
"You draw just one leaf?" I asked.
He looked up without surprise.
"It is enough for a season," he replied.

We sat together for a while in silence. The wind stirred a bamboo fence. His unfinished leaf remained—a universe in miniature.

The Spirit of Small Spaces

One evening in Osaka, I stepped into a convenience store no larger than half my garage back in Pune. Yet within: a bento counter, a wall of manga, an umbrella dispenser, and an aisle of instant noodles boasting flavours that might humble a Parisian sommelier—black garlic, yuzu, wasabi miso. Every square inch sang with purpose.

I asked the young cashier, Yuto, how people managed in such confined spaces. He laughed lightly.

"Big space needs big life," he said. "Small space needs big spirit."
I wanted to embrace him.

Less as Sacred

It struck me, wandering Kyoto at dusk beneath plum-scented air, that this embrace of the small is not just practical—it is philosophical.

In India, we sprawl. Our weddings are oceans of marigolds. Our meals could feed a village. Our homes echo with the steps of imagined guests. We worship abundance. *More is more.*

But in Japan, less is sacred.
A temple bell rings once and is heard for miles.
A single blossom turns the season.
A narrow alley opens into a garden that stills the breath.

Life reduced to essence: a haiku of living.

Just Enough

At a business hotel in Tokyo, my room was scarcely larger than my old study—a bed wedged between two walls. A desk folded like an aircraft tray. The bathroom required choreography. Yet every button, every hinge, every curve of that tiny toilet had a purpose I grew to respect.

And I did not miss a thing.

One morning, I bought a porcelain dish from a small shop tucked behind a shrine—no signage, only a chime at the door. The plate was glazed in sky-blue, just big enough to hold a thought.

"This is for pickles," the shopkeeper said, bowing as she wrapped it tenderly.

I nodded. But silently I whispered:
No, this is for remembering.

When I return to India, it will sit on my dining table. My granddaughter will laugh and ask,
"That's too small, Jeje. What's it for?"

And I will smile and answer:
"It's for just enough."

The God of Small Things

In that dish, I will remember the country that restored something in me I hadn't known was broken. A place where size is not status, silence is not awkward, and attention to the smallest things is both art and worship.

Call it restraint. Call it wisdom.
I call it the God of Small Things.

Epilogue

Lantern on the stream –
a bell fades into twilight,
ink dries, train departs.

It is said that some places let you arrive, while a few let you belong. Rarer still are the places that borrow you, holding you in safekeeping. Japan did this to me.

On my last night, the river wore a necklace of lanterns. Children pressed paper into wooden frames, elders cupped flames against the wind. A woman with a camellia in her hair placed one in my hand. "For whom?" she asked. I left the card blank. The river would know.

Japan resisted being reduced to destination or itinerary. It offered a different grammar: attention before understanding, reverence before explanation. First, small courtesies—bow here, shoes there, silence now. Then, harder lessons—how to sit with ambiguity, to live with beauty that does not announce itself, to let the tilt of a room or the breath of a stranger change your own.

The island lent me things: a slower posture, steps measured like stone; patience for trains that arrive as promised; a practice of ink that dries into truths you cannot revise. In izakaya alleys, chopsticks clinked like bells, steam rose as essays on air, and strangers poured sake with the grammar of enough. Elsewhere, a bamboo grove remembered winds I could not hear. In Hiroshima, silence disallowed metaphor; paper cranes multiplied into the mathematics of grief. Some shapes, I learned, will never fold.

Borrowing carries obligation. To travel without reverence is to counterfeit memory; to write without listening is to counterfeit truth. If Japan borrowed me, I must return myself changed.

On the platform at dusk, the Shinkansen arrived like a clean line of intention—its nose white as unfinished paper, its poise the pause at the end of a brushstroke. Departures here felt less like endings than chords: lantern, bell, ink, rail. Each a liturgy of motion, of memory, of leaving without erasure.

I used to think understanding would arrive as correct answers—why this word, that gesture, those rituals. Instead, comprehension came as form: the way a tea bowl warms the hands before the lips; the arc of a bow that begins with breath; a garden that edits the world until moss becomes a sentence and stone, a clause. Meaning moved from nouns to verbs. Japan is not what it is—it is what it does around you, until you begin to do it too.

When asked what I took back, I list objects: a tenugui, a toy, a small brass bell, among a few others. But these are evasions. What I took was the habit of looking longer. Of treating light as something stewarded, not consumed. Of granting silence a seat at the table. Of letting doors be made of paper so that even closing them feels like listening.

And yet goodbyes here prove slippery. You leave physically—visa expires, flights are booked—but Japan lingers. You find yourself bowing to a kettle, hearing cicadas in your sleep, missing things you never fully understood: the pause before an answer, the architecture of a convenience store bento, the beauty of decay. The country has not released me; it has loaned itself, like a book never meant to be finished.

So this is less a conclusion than an unfinished postcard. Smudged stamps, running ink, but stories intact—folded between memory and dream, essay and echo.

Somewhere, a lantern drifts downstream, carrying a blank card. Somewhere, a train threads from one city to another, its hum braided with a temple bell. Somewhere, a vending machine glows softly, unaware we are gone.

Because in truth, we are not.

Ink dries on the page,
a train hums into the night—
story without end.

❅

Appendix A:

Popular Tourist Spots: Tokyo

Historical & Cultural Attractions

1. Sensō-ji Temple (Asakusa) – Tokyo's oldest and most beloved temple, marked by the iconic Kaminarimon Gate and the bustling Nakamise shopping street.
2. Meiji Shrine (Harajuku) – A serene forested sanctuary dedicated to Emperor Meiji and Empress Shōken, offering a rare stillness in the heart of the city.
3. Imperial Palace & East Gardens – The residence of Japan's Emperor, with beautifully landscaped gardens open to the public.
4. Tokyo National Museum (Ueno) – The country's oldest and largest museum, housing treasures of Japanese art and artefacts from across Asia.
5. Edo-Tokyo Museum – A vivid journey through the transformation of Edo into modern Tokyo, blending models, exhibits, and immersive reconstructions.

Modern Landmarks

6. Tokyo Skytree (Sumida) – Japan's tallest tower, with panoramic observation decks and breathtaking views across the metropolis.
7. Tokyo Tower (Minato) – A red-and-white icon inspired by the Eiffel Tower, offering sweeping city vistas.

8. Roppongi Hills & Mori Tower – A cultural hub combining an observation deck, a contemporary art museum, designer shopping, and vibrant nightlife.
9. Shibuya Crossing – The world-famous "scramble," where thousands of pedestrians cross in a single, choreographed rush of humanity.
10. Shinjuku Gyoen National Garden – A vast and tranquil park blending Japanese, English, and French landscape designs.

Pop Culture & Shopping Districts

11. Akihabara – The electric capital of anime, manga, gaming, and otaku culture.
12. Harajuku & Takeshita Street – A youthful stage for fashion, cosplay, street food, and vibrant self-expression.
13. Shinjuku – Skyscrapers, shopping, nightlife, and the busiest train station in the world.
14. Ginza – Tokyo's luxury showcase, where flagship boutiques and fine dining meet old-world elegance.
15. Odaiba – A futuristic entertainment island featuring teamLab Borderless, the life-sized Gundam statue, and sprawling shopping complexes.

Parks & Outdoor Attractions

16. Ueno Park & Zoo – Museums, spring cherry blossoms, and Japan's oldest zoo in one expansive cultural district.
17. Yoyogi Park – A beloved green escape near Meiji Shrine, alive with picnics, performers, and seasonal festivals.

18. Sumida River Cruise – A leisurely boat ride revealing Tokyo's skyline and bridges from the water's perspective.

✹ Unique Experiences

19. Tsukiji Outer Market – A vibrant maze of fresh seafood stalls, street food vendors, and culinary tools.
20. Toyosu Fish Market – The modern successor to Tsukiji, offering sushi restaurants and an observation deck to watch tuna auctions.
21. Ghibli Museum (Mitaka) – A whimsical tribute to Studio Ghibli, where animation meets imagination.
22. TeamLab Planets Tokyo (Toyosu) – A fully immersive digital art installation where light, water, and movement transform into living canvases.
23. Omoide Yokocho (Shinjuku) – Narrow alleyways lined with smoky yakitori stalls and nostalgic bars.
24. Golden Gai (Shinjuku) – A warren of tiny, atmospheric bars, each with its own eccentric theme and community of regulars.

✨ *Tokyo offers not just sights, but experiences — temples and towers, alleys and art, lantern-lit shrines and neon-lit streets. Each spot is less a destination than a portal: into history, into imagination, into the city's ever-shifting soul.*

❄

Appendix B:

Popular Tourist Spots: Kyoto

1. Iconic Temples & Shrines

- Fushimi Inari Taisha – Famous for its thousands of vermilion torii gates winding up Mount Inari.
- Kinkaku-ji (Golden Pavilion) – A Zen temple gilded in gold leaf, mirrored in a tranquil pond.
- Ginkaku-ji (Silver Pavilion) – Celebrated for its refined simplicity and a beautiful moss garden.
- Kiyomizu-dera – A UNESCO World Heritage site with a vast wooden stage overlooking cherry and maple trees.
- Ryōan-ji – Renowned for its minimalist rock garden and timeless Zen aesthetics.
- Tō-ji Temple – Known for its five-story pagoda (Japan's tallest) and lively monthly flea markets.

2. Traditional Districts

- Gion District – Kyoto's famous geisha quarter, with lantern-lit streets, teahouses, and wooden facades.
- Pontocho Alley – A narrow riverside lane lined with atmospheric eateries, some offering dining with views over the Kamogawa River.
- Higashiyama District – A preserved historic quarter with winding lanes such as Ninenzaka and Sannenzaka, steeped in old-world charm.

3. Palaces & Castles

- Kyoto Imperial Palace – Once home to Japan's emperors, now surrounded by a spacious public park.
- Nijō Castle – A UNESCO site distinguished by its ornate interiors and ingenious "nightingale floors," which chirp underfoot to guard against intruders.

4. Zen Gardens & Scenic Walks

- Philosopher's Path – A contemplative canal walk lined with cherry trees, especially enchanting in spring.
- Arashiyama Bamboo Grove – An ethereal forest of soaring bamboo, with nearby temples, a monkey park, and riverboat rides.
- Tenryu-ji Temple (Arashiyama) – A UNESCO-listed Zen temple framed by exquisite landscape gardens and mountain views.

5. Seasonal & Nature Highlights

- Kurama and Kibune – Mountain villages offering riverside shrines, forest trails, and hot springs.
- Kifune Shrine – Famous for its lantern-lined stone steps, especially atmospheric in summer and winter.
- Eikandō Temple – Celebrated for its fiery autumn foliage and special night illuminations.
- Heian Shrine & Garden – Marked by its massive torii gate and expansive gardens, ideal for leisurely spring strolls.

6. Cultural Experiences

- Kyoto International Manga Museum – A paradise for manga enthusiasts, with shelves of titles from Japan and beyond.

- Nishiki Market – Known as *Kyoto's Kitchen,* a lively arcade packed with food stalls, fresh produce, and culinary shops.
- Tea Ceremony Experiences – Participate in a traditional tea ceremony in a Gion teahouse or a restored *machiya* townhouse.

✨ *Kyoto is a city where time folds: vermilion gates meet moss gardens, geisha quarters meet bamboo groves, and centuries-old rituals continue to breathe in the present. To walk here is to move between history and living art.*

❆

Appendix C:
Popular Tourist Spots: Osaka

1. Food & Nightlife Districts

- Dōtonbori – Osaka's most iconic entertainment district, ablaze with neon lights, the famous Glico running man, and endless street food delights like takoyaki and okonomiyaki.
- Shinsekai & Tsutenkaku Tower – A retro neighbourhood evoking the Showa era, with local eateries, pachinko parlours, and nostalgic charm.
- Kuromon Ichiba Market – Known as *Osaka's Kitchen*, a lively market serving fresh seafood, wagyu skewers, and everyday delicacies.

2. Historic Landmarks

- Osaka Castle – A restored feudal stronghold housing a museum, surrounded by a vast park that is lovely during cherry blossom season.
- Shitennō-ji Temple – One of Japan's oldest Buddhist temples, founded in the 6th century by Prince Shōtoku.
- Sumiyoshi Taisha Shrine – Celebrated for its unique architectural style and the graceful arched Sorihashi Bridge.

🎡 3. Family-Friendly Attractions

- Universal Studios Japan (USJ) – A world-class theme park with The Wizarding World of Harry Potter, Super Nintendo World, Minions, and blockbuster rides.
- Osaka Aquarium Kaiyukan – Among the world's largest aquariums, featuring a massive central tank with whale sharks and diverse marine life from the Pacific Rim.
- Tempozan Giant Ferris Wheel – Soaring views of Osaka Bay, located near the aquarium and Tempozan Marketplace.

🛍 4. Shopping & Pop Culture

- Amerikamura (*Amemura*) – Osaka's answer to Harajuku, a vibrant hub of youth fashion, street art, and Western-inspired trends.
- Nipponbashi (Den Den Town) – The city's centre for electronics, anime, manga, and otaku culture.
- Umeda Sky Building – Twin towers with a futuristic design and the Floating Garden Observatory offering panoramic 360° views.
- Shinsaibashi Shopping Arcade – A bustling covered street blending international brands, Japanese boutiques, and lively cafés.

🏞 5. Parks & Scenic Areas

- Osaka Tenmangū & Tenjinbashi-suji Shopping Street – Visit the historic shrine, then explore Japan's longest covered shopping street.

- Nakanoshima Park – A riverside green oasis with a rose garden and elegant European-style architecture.
- Minoo Park (Minoh) – A nature escape just outside the city, featuring forest trails, a picturesque waterfall, and the seasonal treat of deep-fried maple leaves in autumn.

🚆 6. Nearby Day Trips

- Nara – Just 45 minutes away; home to the Great Buddha at Tōdai-ji, Nara Park's free-roaming deer, and the lantern-lit Kasuga Shrine.
- Kobe – A cosmopolitan port city renowned for Kobe beef, mountain ropeways, and waterfront views.
- Sakai – Known for its master-crafted Japanese blades, ancient kofun burial mounds, and tea culture linked to Sen no Rikyū.

✨ *Osaka is often called "Japan's Kitchen," but it is also a city of contrasts – neon and nostalgia, castles and cuisine, riverside gardens and soaring towers. It welcomes you with flavour, humour, and a warmth that lingers long after you leave.*

❆

Appendix D:

Popular Tourist Spots: Hiroshima

🕊 Historical & Memorial Sites

1. Hiroshima Peace Memorial Park – A vast green space dedicated to the victims of the 1945 atomic bombing, with monuments and memorials for reflection and remembrance.
2. Atomic Bomb Dome (Genbaku Dome) – A UNESCO World Heritage Site, preserved as it stood near the hypocentre of the blast, a haunting symbol of resilience and peace.
3. Hiroshima Peace Memorial Museum – Powerful and deeply moving exhibitions recount the events of August 6, 1945, and their aftermath.
4. Children's Peace Monument – Inspired by Sadako Sasaki, a young girl who folded paper cranes in hope of recovery; thousands of cranes continue to be offered here in her memory.

⛩ Cultural & Spiritual Sites

5. Itsukushima Shrine (Miyajima Island) – Famous for its "floating" vermilion torii gate at high tide; a UNESCO World Heritage Site, easily reached by ferry from Hiroshima city.
6. Daishō-in Temple (Miyajima) – A revered hillside temple with hundreds of statues, scenic paths, and a tranquil spiritual atmosphere.

7. Hiroshima Castle (Carp Castle) – Rebuilt after the war, this castle now houses a museum and is encircled by a moat and cherry blossoms each spring.

Parks & Scenic Areas

8. Shukkeien Garden – A classical Japanese landscape garden with a central pond, tea houses, and seasonal blossoms.
9. Mount Misen (Miyajima Island) – A sacred mountain with panoramic views, accessible by ropeway and short hikes.
10. Hijiyama Park – A hilltop park offering sweeping city views and home to the Hiroshima City Museum of Contemporary Art.

Museums & Culture

11. Hiroshima Museum of Art – A refined collection of European and Japanese modern art, including works by Monet, Picasso, and Van Gogh.
12. Hiroshima City Museum of Contemporary Art (MOCA) – Showcasing Japanese and international contemporary art, with a focus on post-1945 works.

Local Experiences

13. Okonomimura – A lively building filled with eateries specialising in Hiroshima-style *okonomiyaki*, the city's signature savoury pancake.
14. Hondōri Shopping Arcade – A bustling pedestrian street lined with shops, cafés, and local specialities.

✨ *Hiroshima is a city of memory and renewal – its monuments carry the weight of history, its gardens and shrines embody timeless beauty, and its food and streets pulse with everyday joy. To walk here is to witness resilience woven into the fabric of daily life.*

❄

Appendix E:
Useful Addresses for the Vegetarian Travellers

(Tokyo, Kyoto, Osaka, Hiroshima — verified spots serving vegetarian-friendly noodles, tofu, okonomiyaki, or set meals)

TOKYO

T's Tantan Tokyo Station
Vegan ramen with bold sesame broth, tofu, and greens
JR Tokyo Station, Keiyo Street, B1F
https://ts-restaurant.jp/tantan/

Komaki Shokudo (Asakusa)
Vegan soba, traditional plant-based sets
5-20-8 Asakusa, Taito City, Tokyo

Ain Soph Ripple (Harajuku)
Plant-based burgers, Japanese curry, noodle bowls
3-15-8 Jingumae, Shibuya-ku, Tokyo
https://ain-soph.jp/ripple/

KYOTO

Yudofu Sagano
Temple-style yudofu (simmered tofu)
45 Sagatenryuji Susukinobabacho, Ukyo Ward, Kyoto

Mumokuteki Café (Gion/ Teramachi)
Vegetarian udon, soba, Kyoto veggies
261 Motomachi, Nakagyo Ward, Kyoto
https://mumokuteki.com/ cafe/

Vegans Café and Restaurant (Fushimi Inari)
Organic tofu steaks, vegan ramen
5-1 Fukakusa Ichinotsubocho, Fushimi Ward, Kyoto
https://veganscafe.com/

OSAKA

Ramen Papapapapine
Vegan yuzu ramen—light and citrusy
5-9-8 Nishinakajima, Yodogawa-ku, Osaka

Ukihashi (Hotel Granvia Osaka)
Vegetarian kaiseki-inspired set menus
3-1-1 Umeda, Kita-ku, Osaka

HIROSHIMA

Shanti Vegan Café
Vegan curry, simmered veggies, matcha soy milk
3-23-4 Otemachi, Naka Ward, Hiroshima

Nagata-ya
Okonomiyaki—prepared vegetarian by request (kombu stock)
1-7-19 Otemachi, Naka Ward, Hiroshima
https://nagata-ya.jp/

Quick Tips for Vegetarian Travel in Japan

☑ Learn key phrases:
"I don't eat meat or fish" → *Niku to sakana wa tabemasen.*
"I am vegetarian" → *Watashi wa bejitarian desu.*
"No dashi (fish stock), please" → *Dashi nashi de onegaishimasu.*

☑ Watch for hidden fish:
Common broths use bonito flakes (katsuobushi) — ask if broth is kombu/shiitake-based.

☑ Use apps:
The HappyCow app works well in Japan for up-to-date listings. Google Maps reviews in Japanese often include helpful comments

☑ Department stores and convenience stores:
Basement food halls often have clear labels. Look for:

🍙 Onigiri with umeboshi (plum), konbu (seaweed), takana (pickled greens)

🍢 Oden stalls (but check the broth)

🍢 Mochi and rice sweets

☑ Accept kindness:
If a chef or server offers to modify something, accept graciously. It is part of *omotenashi*, which means hospitality of the heart.

❋

Appendix F:

Glossary of Japanese Words and Phrases

◇ Greetings & Common Expressions

- Konnichiwa – "Hello" or "Good afternoon." A standard daytime greeting.
- Ohayō gozaimasu – "Good morning" (polite).
- Konbanwa – "Good evening."
- Sayonara – "Goodbye." Often used for longer or more permanent farewells.
- Itadakimasu – Said before eating; "I humbly receive." Expresses gratitude for food and those who prepared it.
- Gochisōsama deshita – Said after a meal; "Thank you for the feast."
- Arigatō / Arigatō gozaimasu – "Thank you" / "Thank you very much."
- Sumimasen – "Excuse me" or "I'm sorry." Also used to politely attract attention.
- Onegai shimasu – "Please" (polite), often used in requests or when asking for help.
- Wakarimashita – "I understand" or "Got it."

◇ Cultural & Aesthetic Concepts

- Wabi-sabi — An aesthetic of imperfection, impermanence, and subtle beauty.
- Mono no aware — The gentle poignancy of life's transience; a bittersweet awareness of impermanence.
- Ma — The space between things; silence, pause, or negative space in art, architecture, and conversation.
- Shibui — Quiet, understated elegance; refined simplicity without ostentation.
- Omotenashi — The spirit of wholehearted hospitality, given without expectation of return.
- Tatemae / Honne — *Tatemae* is the public façade or polite exterior; *Honne* is one's true, private feelings.
- Zanshin — A state of relaxed alertness and lingering awareness, often in martial arts.
- Yūgen — A mysterious, profound beauty or subtle grace that transcends explanation.

◇ Daily Life, Food & Rituals

- Onsen — Natural hot-spring bath; a ritual of relaxation and purification.
- Sentō — A public bathhouse, not necessarily spring-fed.
- Furo — Bathtub; part of the traditional Japanese bathing culture.
- Ryokan — Traditional Japanese inn, usually with tatami-mat rooms and communal baths.

- Tatami – Woven straw mats used as flooring in traditional rooms.
- Futon – Traditional bedding laid out at night and folded away in the morning.
- Noren – Fabric dividers hung at shop or restaurant entrances; often symbolic.
- Bento – A Japanese boxed meal, artfully arranged in compartments.
- Okonomiyaki – A savoury pancake of flour, cabbage, and various toppings.
- Sake – Japanese rice wine, served warm or chilled.

◇ **Traditional Arts, Sports & Media**

- Haiku – A three-line poem (5-7-5 syllables) evoking nature, seasonality, and insight.
- Ikebana – The disciplined art of flower arrangement.
- Shodō – Japanese calligraphy, written with brush and ink.
- Kabuki – Classical Japanese theatre with stylised acting and elaborate costumes.
- Noh – Ancient masked theatre combining poetry, music, and subtle movement.
- Sumō – Japan's traditional wrestling, rooted in Shinto ritual.
- Pachinko – A pinball-style arcade game, often linked with gambling.

◇ Spirituality & Philosophy

- Shintō — Japan's indigenous belief system, centred on *kami* (spirits or deities).
- Kami — Spirits of nature, ancestors, or sacred places.
- Torii — A gateway marking the entrance to a Shintō shrine, dividing sacred from secular space.
- Zen — A school of Buddhism emphasising meditation, simplicity, and direct insight.
- Satori — A sudden moment of awakening or enlightenment in Zen practice.
- Butsudan — A household altar for honouring ancestors and Buddha.
- Obon — A Buddhist-Confucian festival honouring ancestral spirits, marked with lanterns and dances.

◇ Time, Nature & Festivals

- Hanami — "Flower viewing," especially of cherry blossoms (*sakura*) in spring.
- Sakura — Cherry blossoms; symbols of fleeting beauty and *mono no aware.*
- Tsukimi — "Moon viewing," an autumn festival honouring the full moon.
- Tanabata — The Star Festival; wishes are written on colourful strips of paper and hung on bamboo.
- Kōyō — Autumn foliage, celebrated for its vivid red and golden leaves.

- Natsu / Aki / Fuyu / Haru – Summer / Autumn / Winter / Spring.

◇ **Other Common Terms in Context**

- Gaijin – "Foreigner." Neutral in form, though sometimes with distant undertones.
- Sensei – "Teacher" or "master" in any discipline, not limited to schoolteachers.
- San – The most common honorific suffix, denoting respect.
- Chan – An affectionate suffix for children, family, or close friends.
- Senpai / Kōhai – Senior/junior in school, work, or social hierarchies.
- Yamato-damashii – "The spirit of Japan": connoting honour, endurance, and resilience.

✨ *This glossary is not exhaustive, but it opens a door into the living language of Japan—phrases that carry not only meaning but memory, ritual, and rhythm. To learn them is not merely to translate, but to borrow the cadence of another way of seeing the world.*

❄

Appendix G:

Sixteen Days Across Japan: A Recommended Itinerary

Sixteen days tracing Japan's quiet motion—from city lights to mountain silence.

Day	Highlights	Notes
D1	Arrival in Tokyo (Narita Terminal 1). Pick up Pasmo and Wi-Fi. Take Narita Express to Shinjuku. Explore Omoide Yokochō, Kabuki-chō, Golden Gai, and the Tokyo Metropolitan Government Building.	Collect Wi-Fi and Pasmo before counter closes. Many *izakayas* open late.
D2	Visit Sensō-ji Temple and Nakamise Street (Asakusa). Akihabara walking tour. Shibuya Crossing and evening *pachinko*.	Compact metro transfers; avoid peak hours.
D3	Tokyo National Museum. Toyosu/Tsukiji Markets. Sushi tasting at local stalls. Afternoon go-kart ride over Rainbow Bridge.	Book go-kart and museum slots in advance; expect crowds on Culture Day.

Day	Highlights	Notes
D4	Meiji Shrine. Guided tour of the Imperial Palace East Gardens. Tea ceremony at Imperial Hotel. Night view from Tokyo Met Gov Bldg.	Palace tours require early online registration.
D5	Bullet train (*Nozomi*) to Kyoto. Walk through Nishiki Market and Ponto-chō Alley. Riverside stroll along the Kamogawa.	Travel time ≈ 2 h 16 m. Try *yuba* and Kyoto street snacks.
D6	Day trip to Uji: Itoh Kyuemon tea store and ceremony at Nakamura Tōkichi Honten.	25 min local train; ideal half-day outing.
D7	Kinkaku-ji (Golden Pavilion). Ryōan-ji Temple and rock garden. Gion district walk.	Lunch on *yudōfu* near Ryōan-ji.
D8	Fushimi Inari Taisha. Philosopher's Path walk via Nanzen-ji to Ginkaku-ji.	Sample *obanzai ryōri, Kyo-yasai,* and Uji green tea.
D9	Train via Nagoya to Takayama. Explore Sanmachi Suji Old Town. Dinner with Hida beef.	Local specialities: *hōba miso, soba,* sake.

Day	Highlights	Notes
D10	Miyagawa Morning Market. Hida Folk Village (*gasshō-zukuri*). Relax in Onsen.	Pack warm layers; chilly weather.
D11	Rail to Osaka. Visit Umeda Sky Building, Kuromon Market, and Dōtonbori street food alleys.	Osaka Amazing Pass for transit and entry savings.
D12	Explore Namba and Shinsaibashi Shopping Arcade. Visit Shitennō-ji Temple.	Ideal half-day urban walk.
D13	*Nozomi* to Hiroshima. Peace Memorial Park, Atomic Dome, and downtown evening.	Try oysters, *anago*, and *momiji-manjū*.
D14	Shukkei-en Garden and Mitaki-dera Temple. Dinner at Okonomimura (Hasshō).	Early arrival for temple views and crowd avoidance.
D15	Return to Tokyo (Shibuya). Yamanote Line loop. Evening in Centre Gai and Shibuya Scramble.	4-h journey from Hiroshima; reserve a seat.
D16	Final shopping and *omiyage*. Transfer via Narita Express or Airport Bus.	Confirm flight terminal and tax-free collection time.

Rail & Transport

Shinkansen: Nozomi (fastest) · Hikari (JR Pass) · Kodama (local)
Regional: Ltd. Hida Express (Takayama Line) · Hida Wide View ticket

IC Cards: ICOCA (Kansai) · Suica/Pasmo (Kantō)

Weather · Early November

Tokyo · Kyoto · Osaka: 10 – 20 °C (50 – 68 °F) · mild days / cool nights
Takayama: 2 – 11 °C (36 – 52 °F) · possible snow flurries

Packing Essentials

Layered clothing · warm jacket · scarf · comfortable shoes · adapter (Type A/B) · umbrella · power bank · passport · JR Pass · camera · refillable bottle · snacks

❄